"Masih's stories are minimally but skillfully detailed . . . giving extra weight to simple, recurring phenomena like water and color ('the evening's August melon light'). Striking and resonant, this collection should prove memorable . . ."
—*Publishers Weekly*

"Whether on a car ride, Coney Island—in Europe, or Appalachia, the stories in this collection are like eloquent journeys. *Where the Dog Star Never Glows* illuminates, gracefully, with keenness; with a sharp eye for emotion, and a zoom into the senses, Tara Masih is a talent, and this book is full of heart."
— **Kim Chinquee**, author of *OH BABY* and *Pretty*

"Within each of these stories lies a surprise at the turn of the page. Sometimes subtle, sometimes not, but Masih always has a surprise waiting. This is a wonderful debut collection, which travelers should bring along in their backpacks or suitcases and savor in those moments of solitude."
— **Jeff Talarigo**, author of *The Pearl Diver* and *The Ginseng Hunter*

"These stories travel the world to explore a terrain more mysterious and fulfilling than place—that of the human mind and heart. The finely crafted prose and acute observations in this collection left an indelible impression on me. *Where the Dog Star Never Glows* marks the arrival of a gifted new writer."
— **Lisa Borders**, author of *Cloud Cuckoo Land,* winner of the Fred Bonnie Memorial Award for Best First Novel

"Masih showcases the breadth of her talent in this slim but powerful volume. . . . [I]t is hard to identify a weak link. Masih's ability to fully inhabit each character, and her strong sense of place and time, make each story a standout in its own way. Masih's especially vivid descriptions of landscape and setting allow the reader to become completely immersed in each of her tales, no matter how brief. This is an excellent collection that should appeal to many readers."
—**Elizabeth Schulenburg**, *BookLoons Reviews*

ALSO BY TARA L. MASIH

The Rose Metal Press Field Guide to Writing Flash Fiction, Ed.

WHERE THE DOG STAR NEVER GLOWS

STORIES

Tara L. Masih

*For Stuart –
With many and much
Thanks and much
admiration –
Tara L. Masih 2016*

Press 53
Winston-Salem

Press 53, LLC
PO Box 30314
Winston-Salem, NC 27130

First Edition

Cover art by Benita VanWinkle
www.busybstudio.com

Cover design by Kevin Morgan Watson

Author photos by Michael Gilligan

Library of Congress Control Number: 2009913146

Printed on acid-free paper
ISBN   978-0-9825760-5-2

For my son, Arun,
whose love, creative spirit,
and sweet humor kept me going

in nature there are few sharp lines. . . .
  —A. R. Ammons, from "Corsons Inlet"

CONTENTS

Acknowledgments

"The Guide, the Tourist, and the Animal Doctor," *The Caribbean Writer* (2005)

"Champagne Water," *divide: journal of literature, arts, and ideas* (2006)

"Ghost Dance," *Pangolin Papers* (Winter 2003)

"The Dark Sun," *The Ledge* (Winter 1995); first place, *Ledge* fiction contest

"Say Bridgitte, Please," *Paradise: Four Volumes of Prize-Winning Writing in One Collection* (Florida Literary Foundation, 1994)

"Catalpa," from *Fragile Skins* (The Feral Press, 2006); winner, Carolyn A. Clark Flash Fiction Prize

"Where the Dog Star Never Glows," *Natural Bridge* (Spring 2004)

"Asylum," *Confrontation* (Spring/Summer 2001)

"Sunday Drives," *Pangolin Papers* (Winter 2000)

"Huldi (India, 1990)," *The Indian-American* (1992); reprinted in *Brevity & Echo* (Rose Metal Press, 2006)

"The Sin Eater," *New Millennium Writings* (Winter 1998–99)

"Memsahib," *Colere* (2005)

"Suspended," *The HUB* online (Spring 2007)

"The Burnings," *The Merrimack Literary Review* (2004)

"Turtle Hunting," *Hayden's Ferry Review* (Summer 1990); reprinted in *Brevity & Echo* (Rose Metal Press, 2006)

WHERE THE DOG STAR NEVER GLOWS

The Guide, the Tourist, and the Animal Doctor

The machete sliced through the top of the green coconut. Therese performed her daily task with an assured mixture of force and care—one had to keep the milk inside from spilling. She did this until the small heap of coconuts on the ground beside her became a gathering of shells, open like cups, in the grass before her.

Her morning routine generally went this way—waking with the dawn, helping the children ready their packs, walking them to school, returning to cut down the young, fleshy coconuts, opening them, draining their milk into a bowl, scraping some nutmeg and cinnamon bark on top, stirring, pouring the mixture into the conical corners of sandwich bags, twisting them closed with wire ties. The handmade pops then went into the freezer of her new GE refrigerator, the only major appliance in the house of two rooms, partitioned into three by flowery cotton curtains.

The GE was a source of income in that tropical clime. Having the uncommon ability to freeze things or keep drinks cold for tourists helped supplement her income as a female nature guide. Foreign tourists tended to have a greater trust in the male guides, felt they were more likely to know where they were going and to

1

get their charges there more safely. To compete, women like Therese offered their services for less and, on quiet days, resorted to selling out of their coolers. Therese was proud that her refrigerator—which cost 200 Carib dollars, made up of monthly payments of $5—had a freezer. She was the only guide who could offer the coconut pops, and she was very careful to keep the cooler clean and white and to wash it daily so tourists wouldn't be afraid to eat or drink what came out of it. And if she was hired to guide, she left her cooler safely by the entrance to the trails and took her people to the sulfur pools, grottos, or waterfalls the Dominican islanders now shared with the rest of the world.

On this morning, Therese packed her cooler with Coca-Cola and pops and walked a mile up the road toward the Trafalgar Falls entrance.

"Hallo, Therese," Jemma called from her roadside garden.

"Jemma, good day, huh?"

"You see dat couple go by? Some folk headin' up to da falls in a rental. You get goin', you be the first to pass by today." The older woman stood between her tall hibiscus bushes, her delicate hand flapping like a bird's wing.

The road slithered to the right and then abruptly to the left, at the end of which was a small cantina closed down for the impending rainy season. The hand-painted wooden sign that marked the rain forest trail intercepted the sun's rays and sent a slant of shade over a dusty car. Most rental cars on the island were pitted with rust and dented by rocks, the companies not wanting to constantly repair the damage caused by the rutted, neglected roads, and this car was no exception.

Therese put on her seller's grin and proceeded to woo the couple just getting out. She happily accepted, from the man who introduced himself as Paul and his wife as Toni, 20 U.S. dollars. (She could exchange them later for more Carib dollars in Rouseau.) As she pocketed the bill she assessed their clothing. Both wore blindingly white shorts and sneakers, collared short-sleeve shirts and sun visors in pastel shades, and mirrored sunglasses. He had a camcorder slung over one shoulder and a 35 mm camera over the other. She carried a leather purse.

"You want to carry all that stuff?"

The woman clung more tightly to her purse. "We can't leave them in the car."

Therese shrugged. She set down her cooler at the base of the sign with enough emphasis to send up small puffs of the same pale roadside dirt that clung to the car. She moved forward to the entrance. Overhanging branches and vines competed to block out the daylight, and ground lizards scattered in panic at the sight and sound of intruders.

The best guides sense quickly whom they're being paid to lead and match their chatter and stride. Impatient guides sometimes leave their charges way behind to struggle on their own along treacherous, volcanic ledges or over fast-moving rivers, and as a result more than one tourist had taken a fatal misstep off a steep cliff walk. Therese always controlled her pace, looked for the firmest, safest foundations for her customers' often inappropriately shod feet. Her own climbing technique, goatlike and instinctive to all islanders, allowed her to step in bare feet or sandals on rounded rocks made black with water and slippery with green moss.

When she turned to help the woman over a boulder almost as wide as the river that washed around it, the woman's purse slipped and splashed into the water. Therese leapt down and retrieved the dripping bag. Her customer took it with thanks and a pinched expression of guilt.

By the time they reached the falls, the couples' shins were grazed with pink-red stripes and the blossomings of purple bruises. But Therese, holding out a helping hand to both, had to admire their lack of complaining and determination to reach the interior.

"I hear something," the man said after a pause to settle his breathing.

"Yes, just a little more and . . ." Therese lifted her hands, palms up, to the forest scene, proud of the water that exploded from bedrock and fed into pools cradled in limestone. Sulfur springs from below fed into the same pools, making them warm, invigorating, restorative. A few local families lounged on the ledges; a mother held her chubby baby under the arms and dipped his legs into the cloudy water.

The woman named Toni looked at her husband, and he nodded. His face was florid, sweat running from his hairline and specking the collar of his shirt. They removed their muddy sneakers and socks and climbed to the first ledge, set their feet into a pool. Therese watched their face muscles slacken, the corners of their mouths lift a little. She turned and left them alone.

On the way back to the rental, the couple chatted behind her.

"Therese," the man called forward to her, "we need help with something. We traveled with a friend who brought her cat—"

"*Cat?*"

"Yeah, crazy, huh? But it was the only way we could get her to leave home. Her husband died last year. Well, the darn animal stepped on a fish hook this morning, and it went right into the paw. That's why she's not here. We told her we'd ask around for a vet."

Therese nodded. "A friend of mine is an animal doctor. Where are you staying?"

"At the Sisserou Resort. She's in the Moon Cottage, up front. That'd be just great. Listen, thanks, much obliged for everything. Worth it, to soak the old toes in that." He held out his hand in good-bye as they reached the car.

The woman tipped her sunglasses to the top of her head to show her eyes and smiled. "That was as beautiful as the guide books said it would be. I'm glad we met you and thank you for rescuing my handbag. Silly me, to take it on a hike. I'll get a fanny pack next time."

After two tries the car revved to life and backed up to turn around. Therese shaded her eyes and waved. A few guides now clustered across the road. Not ready to join them, she sat on her cooler, prepared to let another guide have the first shot at the next rental or taxi that drove up. Hungry, she stood and opened the lid, rifled for a pop. Sitting again, she untangled the tie and took a bite of the cold, crystalline sweetness. A quiet, happy feeling settled on her. She knew from experience that its source began with the connection she had just made, a connection made more valuable by its unlikeliness. The strength and immediacy of the feeling would wear off, so she paid close attention to the moment, to the way the ice melted back to spiced milk as she rolled it in her mouth.

Irvin knew the sound—the soft muffled echoes of bare feet against the scaly, sun-dried wood of his verandah stairs. When he heard the voice—"*Bon jou*, Irvin"—he jumped from his chair, losing his place in his newspaper as the ink-smudged sheets fell from his lap.

"*Bon jou*, Therese." He returned the Creole greeting and smiled as widely as he could. Stepping over the papers, he reached the screen door and opened it till the hinges resisted.

Heads taller than Therese, he looked down at the top of her head as she moved forward and into his home. Her hair, pushed back from her forehead with a cloth band, puffed up like the fan of a peacock's tail. He got a brief whiff of coconut. He let the door back slowly so it wouldn't bang, but stayed near, studying her as she carried out her ritual—a look to the left, a look to the right, then left again, as if searching for something. It was common knowledge in the village that her husband, Ossie, had cheated on her, and Irvin suspected Therese might never believe that there was no one else but her that Irvin wanted, that she would always search the shadows for betrayal.

She turned back to face him, hands to her thick waist. "I need you to go to the Sisserou. A tourist has a cat that needs to have a fish hook removed. Can you go now? It has been hurt since morning. She is in the Moon Cottage."

Irvin, used to her businesslike tone, always tried to lift their casual relationship to another level in the way he would lift the dead weight of an unconscious animal.

"I'll go now. Do you want to come?" he asked, grabbing a few medical supplies from a cabinet and putting them into his *conta*.

Her eyes moved to the left. "No, there's work in the garden, and the children will be home soon."

They said their good-byes at the end of the front path. As Therese turned away he watched her solid figure retreat. He wanted her not for her beauty—her nose was too flat and her knees turned in—but for the way she knew how to walk away from a man. So few women left their men, and most men were able to keep more than one woman under their care. St. Joe, the owner of the local rum shop, boasted *ven*—twenty—girlfriends.

Irvin knew any island woman who had the strength to leave a man to be on her own would stay and love one just as hard. Being a doctor he didn't want for choices, but also being a doctor he understood the fragility of bone and sinew that encompassed the even more fragile organ of the heart. He envisioned Therese's as being wound in intricate, tight, vinelike veins that he would slowly make sense of and unravel.

The blare of a horn sent him off the road into the grasses and ferns, as a truck bursting with banana pickers—hanging off the side, standing on the bumper, crammed into the well—sped past, spraying him with dirt and small pebbles. The vehicle appeared to be on two tires instead of four as it leaned into the hairpin turn. He knew a few pickers and they waved, but the truck disappeared around the bend, too full to stop and give him a lift.

He made it to the hotel within the hour, passing a neighbor, Spider Vaneau. Spider carried a bamboo pole and a bucketful of contraband crayfish from the Boeri River and offered to leave some in the shade of Irvin's verandah.

"Thank you. *Bon apwé midi.*" Irvin was used to such gifts in return for his services—last week he had helped Spider's goat survive a breech birth. Tonight, he'd make a crayfish stew and invite Therese, though she always said no. But it still made him smile to have a reason to talk to her again.

Ms. Jameson tilted her wrist again to check the time. Only a few minutes had ticked by since the last time she'd looked, and a few hours since Paul and Toni had stopped by to inform her that a vet was on the way.

The cat mewled, and she stroked the soft fur back from its head, stroked its side, feeling the stomach's rapid rise and fall as the animal hyperventilated from shock and pain. A rusty fish hook had dug itself into the pad of its right front paw after it had escaped her cottage for the garden.

"There, there," she murmured, and not knowing what else to do, hummed "Rock-a-Bye Baby."

"Hello, Madame." She jumped and turned from the bed to see her screen door completely filled with the contours of a huge, dark, muscular man. He introduced himself as the local animal doctor, and she let him in, playing with the gold cross at her throat as she watched him approach the cat.

"I know it was silly of me to bring him on a trip like this—"

"Not at all," he interrupted. "How could you leave him behind?" He smiled at her and she let out a sigh. Her hand stilled.

"I can see when an animal is loved," he went on casually, holding out his hand, knuckles upward, till it was beneath the cat's nostrils. The cat had lifted itself partially when it heard his voice, but after pulling back a bit, it put its head to the hand and sniffed. After a moment, it settled back and the doctor gathered it by the scruff. Then he took his other arm, slid it under and through the hind legs, and carried the cat on his inner forearm, legs dangling over his wrist.

"I need the sun for better light. Bring a pillowcase."

Ms. Jameson pulled a hotel-white linen off a pillow and followed him outside. The cat's eyes stared in fear and its panting was heavier, but it didn't fight the transfer.

On a garden bench, under an arch of bougainvillea vines that climbed around the trellis frame, the cat was laid down and covered, but for its paw.

"Hold him down."

The doctor pulled off his rustic backpack and opened the basket-weave top. She watched warily as he took out age-darkened pliers, gauze packets, and a small amber glass bottle. Taking the paw, he pushed the barb through the pad's outer sheath of skin. Ms. Jameson felt the cat's muscles jump and resist, so she pressed harder. The point snapped off, then the rest of the hook was pulled out while the doctor also held down the cat and avoided the claws that pushed out in defense.

Ms. Jameson suddenly felt the urge to cry, and let it happen.

"This is a peppermint infusion I make myself." He opened the bottle, poured the infusion over gauze and wiped the paw, then recorked the bottle. "It is a very good antiseptic. Put it on twice daily with these gauze bandages. Bathing the wound in salt water is good, too. And he needs water right away—cold, not icy. He is dehydrated."

She wiped her face quickly and took the small cloudy bottle and paper packets. "How much do I owe you?"

He hesitated. "You are about the same size as a friend of mine. Do you have other shoes to wear here? May I have your sneakers?"

Ms. Jameson almost jumped out of them, she was so surprised. She started to protest, then bit down on her unformed words. He hadn't questioned her feelings for her cat. She would return the favor.

A minute later she stood in her white Tretorn tennis socks, holding the cat's head over her shoulder—the body wrapped in the cotton case like bunting—watching the doctor leave, admiring the solid, veined backs of his calves, wondering at the fate of her Reeboks, and feeling a bit envious of the new owner.

The little battery-operated radio was playing Jah Lee's "En Non Allez." The zouk music filled the dusky air, redolent with the heady mix of almost acrid smoke from evening cook fires and the light perfume of honeysuckle vines. Therese sat at a table, allotting the day's cash into special piles that needed to be stretched through the week. U.S. dollars to be exchanged in one pile, Carib dollars in five other piles. Her daughter, Eve, swayed around the kitchen, lost in the rhythm of the kettle drums. Her little son, Matel, jumped up and down on sturdy legs, no grace, just pounding, ecstatic pleasure.

She left them when she heard a knock. Their end-of-day release receded into the background as she made her way to the door, parting curtains.

"Irvin, *ki sa on vlé*? What do you want?"

"I want you and Eve and Matel to eat with me tonight, and I want you to accept these."

Therese looked down at the sneakers that glowed white like phosphorescent coconut meat in the new twilight. The radio's tinny sounds and the youthful giggles and the mountain frogs' swelling chorus seemed momentarily louder. And then as swift and sweet as the slice of a machete, her heart broke open.

CHAMPAGNE WATER

—

They lie as if they existed in the days when bundling was the custom, only there is no real wooden board between them in the bed, meant to inhibit sexuality, but a space just as hard and thick and impenetrable. The night wind pushes rain through the screen and leaves them both feeling restless, their minds tossing with the black electrical wires outside. Lightning is so close it mimics a strobe, and Jill stares at the black flowers on the wallpaper against the bluish-lit background for the second it's illuminated.

She wants to cry; she doesn't want to cry. She wants to scream; she wants to disappear into the secure oblivion of sleep.

Thunder drowns out his words.

She closes her eyes, tries to forget he spoke.

But Louis is shaking her shoulder. She won't be allowed to disappear yet.

Her arms are filled with a week's worth of homemade frozen dinners.

"You're late," her mother spits out, continuing the unfortunate ritual they must go through every time Jill first arrives at the small blue house where she grew up. Something is always said to keep the reunion from being too pleasant, to keep things in the elderly woman's control. Once it's done, they go on.

"Louis and I are going to Dominica for a week, sort of a last-minute decision. You'll be OK on your own?"

Her mother looks closely, searching. Jill tries to keep masked.

"I'm fine. You worry too much. Go." She nods her graying head in dismissal, sending a hairpin sliding down the slippery satin camisole. Her bun, these days, never stays put. It begins the day at the back of her head, stiff and proud, and ends the day around her shoulders, a coarse ball at the end of a rope that swings with the emphasis of her convictions. Jill no longer fixes it. Her mother doesn't want to admit that it isn't in its proper place.

"I'll call every day."

"Well, do what you want. Now give me a kiss and leave me to watch *Mystery* in peace."

Jill bends to kiss her peach-skin soft face, leaving a temporary dent with her lips. She imagines the impression remains after she leaves this house of poor memories.

Louis takes her hand. She lets it be for a moment, feeling his calluses, the sweat gathered in his lifelines, then pulls it gently away as if it is compelled to point out the small runway they are approaching. Dry grass and dusty palms speed by as the plane begins its frantic, bumpy landing.

Louis steps onto the asphalt, takes a deep, enthusiastic breath of air. "Dominica smells different. Like burning wood, doesn't it?"

Jill's sniff is polite, her mind elsewhere, wondering how she is going to keep up with such optimism, in this place where he's invested so much hope.

With a map that looks like it came off a cereal box to guide them, they follow the single, unmarked road into the interior. The rusty, unkempt rental car creaks and groans, resisting the steep mountain climb. Louis adjusts quickly to driving European style, but Jill still feels they are on the edge of disaster every time he rounds the hairpin turns.

"Look at these mountains. Banana trees growing right up 'em. I never knew bananas grew that way."

Jill stares out the window at the passing view. The jungle is dense, leaving little room for clearings or space. Banana trees of various size sprout from both above and below the paved road, bearing bunches that point upward, defying gravity. Some are encased in blue plastic.

The road levels out to a valley. Pastel-colored shacks, blanched a lighter shade from the tropical sun, settle on rock-strewn earth or bury their stilt foundations into a place that once held an ancient river.

"They grow gardens in cans here." Jill eyes the tins arranged on front steps and windowsills. Some are painted with leftover house paint; some retain the original labels, peeling and pitted. "They look cheery. It's like each flower has its own home."

"I think we're almost there," says Louis. "Keep a lookout for a lodge." Once again they are climbing. To her right, Jill watches a river meet up with the road. It continues to race alongside, clear and blue and frothy, rushing over brown-black boulders.

Facing the river, the lodge rests at the base of the rainforest. Phillip, the manager, greets them with a wide smile and "welcome drinks" of rum punch.

"Whew, this is strong." Jill's head swims almost immediately with the taste of tropical fruit and hard liquor.

"This is great. You arrive hot and sweaty, and they give you a drink. Great way to wind down."

A red-throated hummingbird buzzes around the courtyard garden, from hibiscus bush to persimmon tree, from orchid to orchid. It passes close to Jill's head in a frenzy of motion, speeding with such determination that she ducks against the loud buzzing of wings.

The room is damp, so she agrees to go with Louis to the Emerald Pool. They reach the tourist spot by following wooden boards laid down in a serpentine path through the jungle. The grotto collects the spill from the waterfall that empties into it. Jill strips to her bathing suit and wades into the warm green water, feeling her progress over mossy rocks. They are alone. Louis films her with his camcorder, an old model he bought for their honeymoon in Hawaii.

She wants to get to the falls, and reaching the feathery cascade, she turns to face him. Louis is speaking, but she can't make it out. The falls are too ferocious to stand beneath, so she rests behind the watery curtain on a rock ledge carved into the cliff. She closes her eyes, imagines she is back in her mother's womb—fertile, dark, mossy—the falls a protective barrier—against the outside world of human imperfection, even against the very mother who carries her.

The water-smoothed rock pillows Jill's body, stiff from months of sleepless nights. She wonders about being alone again. After four years of marriage to Louis, even her feelings of fondness are beginning to be watered down, diluted with his seemingly baseless constancy.

She hears the change in water flow. Wet and grinning, he pushes his way through the edge of the falls.

"Nice cave you got here. Mind if I join you?"

She sees he is going to reach for her. She slides away, knowing he's too trusting to even guess she's avoiding his touch.

"It's cold. You stay."

"Hey, put the camcorder on me."

From the bank where their clothes lie on logs, she turns the lens on his large, six-foot figure, now floating in the pool, the green tinting his white skin. She zooms in closer to focus on his face. Partially submerged, he looks far away. And with a start she wonders if she just assumes his thoughts. Where does he go, she wonders, when his mind travels away from her?

The lodge's restaurant, hung with island fabrics in reds and blues for a tent effect, smells of rain and mildew, but the floating candles, cupped in round water vases, flicker from the breezes, making it close and charming. They are the only customers, but for one other, a man who looks to be in his thirties, a dark ponytail resting casually down his back. He looks up from the book he is reading, grins when he sees her studying him.

Louis also catches her look and gestures when he sees the smile. "Why don't you join us? This seems silly, just the three of us . . ."

Jill looks down at the "mountain chicken" being placed before her. She can't help but feel the invitation is a mistake. She picks up one leg of the large frog, its barbecued parts displayed artfully amongst greens and edible flowers.

"Thanks. Ron Cawley." He extends his hand even as he rises to move. Louis shakes it in his hearty way; when the man shakes hers, she feels singed at the touch.

Conversation flows with the fruit punch they order, and Jill finally joins in. Soon, they're discussing a way to save Dominican ecology and economy, in the wake of the banana exporters losing their foothold in the European market. Their guest tells them that exporting orchids is his government-approved project, and that he is researching the right land on which to start.

"But how can you get a whole country, small as it is, to change what they've been doing for generations? What I've seen of this island, most of it's banana trees and sheds and warehouses."

They have lost Louis somewhere in the talk, and Ron half rises as Louis excuses himself for the night. Jill tells him she'll be along soon. Mosquitoes find their way through the slatted screens on the windows and buzz around her ankles. Frogs begin their overwrought mating calls from the bush beneath and up the mountainside that shadows the hotel. Jill stifles a sneeze again, the mildew smell growing stronger with the dewfall. She hasn't talked like this in years, like something matters, hasn't heard passion in someone's voice to raise her own, and she is reluctant to end it.

"It'll be hard. But my people are farmers. We love this volcanic soil. They won't be asked to give that up, just to see that our flowers and plants sell to mainlanders like you, someone who can afford them as a luxury, and pay dearly for that hibiscus over there for your living room, something farmers here push aside when they plant their trees."

"Well, I wish you all the luck."

"Thanks."

The cook and the waitress leave by the front door, and Phillip shakes coins in his register. His perpetual smile is turned off.

As Jill turns sideways to stand, Ron asks, "Have you drunk from the river yet?"

"What river? The one across the street?"

"Yes, the Laudat. We're proud here that you can drink from any moving river or stream. There's nothing like taking a long walk through the hot jungle and kneeling down to take a cold drink into your hand."

"We didn't know."

"Come on."

She avoids Phillip, whose stare is furious, as if it alone could change her mind, and follows Ron out the front door, across the dirt road to the riverbank. The moon is swollen and its brightness highlights the outlines of the boulders and rocks that litter the edge. Hibiscus flowers, following the road's border, have closed their petals for the night, twisted carefully, their veiny undersides exposed. Ron is a silhouette now that she follows cautiously, her sneakers sometimes slipping. He reaches back and grabs her hand, pulls her from rock to rock until they are in the middle of the dark water, on an island of river refuse. Her ears are overwhelmed with the sounds of rapids.

When they reach a calm spot behind a large hill of rock, she watches matter-of-factly as he strips to his underwear. She does the same, enters the cool water that is swirling into a gentle whirlpool.

He circles, telling her to drink. She lowers her chin, takes in the water, surprisingly sweet. For the first time that night they are quiet. He continues to circle her, part of the motion of the whirl, and she treads in the center, turning to watch as he moves, his face going light and shadow as he satellites, water slipping over shoulders, fanning out hair. She throbs, despite the cold, from the intensity of his unswerving gaze, from his primitive silence.

A different sound from those of the rapids and frogs breaks through as droplets begin to fall on her head and the yielding water. She aches for what is coming, but she knows she has to turn away.

The drops become a downpour, and she stumbles to the lodge house. The night has turned, leaving her shivering. Louis wakes when she enters, turns his back to the door, doesn't check on her when, in the bathroom, she screams at the sight of a glossy cockroach the size of her fist. Forget the shower, she thinks, and towels dry over the cement sink.

The mattress is almost as damp as the room. Though she shivers, she stays away from the warmth her husband's body offers. He is awake; she can tell by his back's stiffness, his purposeful lack of movement, his tight breathing.

The rain does its job, pounding the plants and the trees and the soil. The shutters are closed and the chalet's large overhang holds back the sheets of water. Incense, in a ceramic dish on the floor, burns to ward off mosquitoes, sending up woodsy smoke that fills the room, trapped.

Two warm tears fall in perfect lines from the corners of her eyes to her river- and rain-soaked hair.

"Why are you taping that? The fish are just brown river fish."

"I just want to."

Jill leaves her husband videotaping the tank in the dining room. She gives the restaurant, now faded in the daylight, only a cursory glance, finds herself drawn to the riverbank. Ron spoke of leaving early, she remembers, looking to the parking lot where his car should be. No sign is left that he was there, no dry spot on the asphalt. He must have left when it still rained.

The Laudat River now flows with deathly force—a muddy, obscene brown ploughing forward tree trunks and debris. A fur-covered carcass sweeps by, too fast to identify. The path she took last night is flooded over.

Louis now stands beside her.

"I can't get over how brown it is today. It was so clear yesterday. You think this kills the fish?" he asks.

"I don't know."

Silence follows them along the coastal, windward road, headed north. This is how it's been lately, their marriage. Quiet. Isolation. Only today Jill senses Louis's silence is not neutral. He is angry. As angry as he knows how to be. Do I care? she wonders. Maybe this is good.

The jagged headlands of the northwest coast rise high above sea level, rusty cliffs that meet cerulean waters, which power their way into coves and inlets, sending spray rocketing. The Carib territory appears wild and undiscovered. She can see why the Indians managed to fight off Europeans for so long—no ship could enter these waters. Even Columbus only sailed by, just time enough to baptize it "Dominica" after the day on which he passed.

She is disappointed to see that the few huts and kiosks advertising Carib crafts and crab backs are all closed for the off-season. Up ahead, a cement building, washed in aqua, holding up a bright red Coke sign, looks open. Louis takes his foot off the gas.

"Thirsty?" His anger reduces the question to one obligatory word.

He parks the rental in the sandy apron of hard-packed dirt just outside the dooryard. Chickens scatter, clucking nervously. A small cooler inside holds hand-chiseled ice blocks and soda. They pick out two orange Juce-Es, and Louis wipes ice water from the bottles, pushing the water to the dirt floor. Phillip had told them before they checked out that 15 years ago a tourist drove through the territory, his rental car stoned the entire way by the Indians. Jill is relieved that the shopkeeper, while not exactly friendly, is not hostile, either.

The day remains a milky-white haze as they approach the north end, the hillside villages growing into busy roadside towns. Villagers tend cooking fires in the dust by the road, roasting corn in its husk to sell for a small price. Jill sees the universal glow of TV sets through open doors, villagers on radiophones. Rastafarian influence is everywhere—graffiti, posters, dress, hair. Men sit along the road on fences and benches, too stoned to work. "The locals, like your American Indians, can't tolerate liquor. You'll see that more in Calibeshie. Don't go into their bars or homes. They can get violent. And don't wear a lot of jewelry," was Phillip's last piece of advice.

Despite the ocean, bright bougainvillea vines, trailing smoke from cookfires, the afternoon drags by. Jill tires from the strain between them and the rough ride around cliff corners. Louis leans on his horn before approaching a blind turn, but still they are almost hit head-on by trucks carrying banana pickers from the fields. Louis's hard silence, the frightened starts, and the humidity take their toll.

It is a small island, and they have made the half-sweep by 5 p.m. to reach their next bungalow on the eastern beach of Picard, an old coconut plantation. She is relieved to see wire-mesh screens on the windows and a clean bath, though the mattress is once again damp.

"At least it doesn't smell moldy," she comments, pressing her hand to it, releasing the moisture.

Once again they fill one of only two occupied tables in the outdoor restaurant. Four men sit, leaning on their table, drinking and bantering good-naturedly. Their spirited loudness accentuates the heavy silence between Jill and Louis, who concentrate hard on finishing their fried chicken and plantains, and *tannia*—a potato-like root.

The night air is cooling down. The bungalow's path along the beach is of gray volcanic sand, still wet from the previous night's storm and now black in the darkness. Jill is used to being the one who breaks the discord. Tonight she lets things be, hoping he will give up, her mind already planning the future.

He opens the porch door and holds it for her, but doesn't follow. He looks uncomfortable, tense between the brows, as if he is dropping her off at her home, a place where he doesn't belong. She frowns in question.

"You made up your mind before we came, didn't you. You're not going to try. You went off with that guy on purpose."

"Nothing happened, I—"

"So what? We're still married, aren't we? Aren't you supposed to care about me, even if you don't love me?"

They stare at each other, eyes wider. They haven't voiced this before.

He leaves; the screen door slaps the space in front of her.

She tries to sleep in the twist of damp sheets, alone, unable to avoid her own heat and remorse. Winds from the south bring heavy smells of sulfur, reminding all that the island was once in the belly of the earth. She thinks of calling her mother. After the international codes are dialed, the rings go unanswered. She puts the old phone back in its cradle, slowly, feeling rejected somehow. A faint heartbeat of disco carries over the rise and fall of the bay's surf, from some island nightspot.

Her porch light only cuts the outside dark by a few feet. Maybe another storm coming. She is reminded of a time in Maine when she lived alone, and a hurricane shook her third-floor apartment, sending potted begonias and pansies careening around her roof deck. She sat in a rocking chair in the middle of the room, rocking frantically, feeling as if she were the only one left on the planet. The phone lines dead, the neighbors away—the desolation was unbearable.

She spies Louis on the dock in front of the restaurant, a shape in the globe of light cast by the pier lamp. Reaching him, she sits gingerly on the rough-hewn boards.

"You chose me," he accuses.

"I know."

He is looking at the moving water below. Schools of fish hover in the pool of light, suspended, all looking attached to the same line.

"Watch," Louis says, and lifts his hand.

The fish disappear instantly in a flash of iridescence, in one common direction.

"They're called needlefish. The waiter told me they're attracted to the light, maybe for the bugs. . . . Amazing, isn't it, how they all face the same way, and move like they're of one mind?"

The fish gather under the spotlight again for a few seconds, then nervously dart away. They see the larger shadow of a fish pass by, a larger predator attracted to the needlefish and their blue beacon of color.

Watching reminds Jill of when she first met Louis, so different from the men she'd dated before. It took awhile before she let him in; steady rides had always bored her. But his touch somehow calmed her and it was as if he'd blown in after the hurricane, landing on her steps at just the right time. Their summer dates consisted of frozen yogurt, a blanket, and the stars. He liked to take her to the open spaces of meadows and golf courses and point out constellations, stars, planets. He'd test her, and by fall she knew them all—the dagger of Orion, the flat band of the Milky Way.

She looks up now, but the stars are all out of place.

"What do you think you can get from a stranger, Jill? Think about that, and what it says about you."

Jill hears tears in his voice for the first time in the five years they've known each other. She suddenly realizes they aren't just talking. They're not just breaking up a romance, but a way of life. And a ritualistic promise. She feels millions of nerve endings in her face go wild, panicky.

The moon clouds over as he leaves her alone with the mosquitoes and the fish and the ocean moving beneath her.

The rain comes again that night, with lightning and thunder just as anywhere else, but the sound of the monsoon downpour is different. It is hard, punishing, slapping the unprepared ground, tugging at the large, shiny, tropical leaves and the fringes of dry palms, curling down the round trunks, the downspouts, the telephone poles, feeling its way into the broken pieces of the earth and eventually finding its way back to the broiling ocean.

"You miss the beauty." Their guide pauses, leans over his wooden oars. He points out certain trees, then continues rowing. "They bloom earlier."

Jungle trees drip to the water, hung with strands of twisted lianas, and land crabs dive from cave shelters dug into the hardened mud banks as their rowboat passes. The guide pulls on the oars passively, barefoot and bored, strong and beautifully defined like the rest of the islanders. The Indian River is mostly used as a vehicle for floating banana barges from the fields upriver to the cargo boats waiting at the mouth of Portsmouth Bay, but it allows itself to provide a living for those who can afford a boat, or share one, to tempt tourists for a few Carib dollars.

At the point where the banks are closest, and the trees above touch and intertwine to form a canopy, a spot has been cleared and an enormous grass hut erected. Beneath it waits a young bartender, ready to catch the rope, help them ashore, and serve them coconut drinks from a large red cooler. The drink is small and expensive and served in white plastic cups, but is creamy and fresh, with strong island rum.

"Go, walk," their guide forcefully instructs, and he himself disappears down a path leading away from the clearing.

Obediently they carry their cups and head down another path, carpeted with dark shadows and a mosaic of sunshine penetrating the ancient branches above. A sound, almost like rain, follows them, as myriad lizards scatter in the dry undergrowth.

"Most women would be squealing right now," Louis remarks flatly, a carefully neutral observation. His whole manner since two nights ago has changed. It is as if they are acquaintances, agreeing to finish out the last two days of a failed journey. Jill feels a little disoriented, sometimes almost dizzy as the ground beneath her seems to breathe a huge sigh. She is hurt by this new husband, his about-face setting off some sort of imbalance.

Suddenly blinded, she puts her hand up to shade her eyes from the sun. They are now on the edge of a banana farm. The trees, barely taller than she, are planted haphazardly, without the puritan need for alignment and order—some dead, some living, some living and bearing fruit. A light wind rustles the parchment leaves, the sound like twigs crackling in a dying fire.

They haven't seen such bright sunlight in several days, and Jill leans against a tree, holding her face upward. A click. She opens her eyes. Louis has snapped a shot of her. She stares, puzzled. Lately she has stopped taking pictures of him, but she brings her camera along anyway, for to leave it behind would make more of an obvious statement.

"Why did you take that?"

He shrugs. "I liked the composition."

They are running out of time. The final days loom ahead, and suddenly Jill becomes scared. She senses Louis's fear, too, and with a friendly guide they rush from one tourist spot to another, trying to reclaim some normalcy and avoid being alone together. As she stands watch over a small pool of boiling sulfide water—a natural hot spring, nestled among high grasses, gray and uninviting—she wonders when that precise moment is when you know that the promise of the death-do-you-part relationship cannot be kept. And hiking up the clouded mountain trail to the Boeri Lake, she watches his back and mourns the loss of physical attraction she once felt for him. She is hungry to feel that again, dreams of it. But small doubts are bringing insecurities to the surface—what if it's just a matter of commitment? Her mother would say her generation wasn't taught that word, flirted with it but never settled on it.

On the trip down the mountain, after a meal of fish and bread fruit by the lake, they pass a tall, dark woman who stops to talk to their guide in island Creole. The heavy makeup surprises Jill, out in the wild, by the rusty stain of a mineral stream. Then she notices the eyes are too round, the throat too muscular and protruding.

"Was that—?"

"*Oui*," the guide answers, explaining that she is one of the island's few men that live as women. "She met a man last year, from Guadeloupe. He fall in love with her. Big love. He go back to his island for work, and was suppose to return for her to be his bride. Dat man found out she was a man, did not come back. She be heartbroken."

Jill looks behind them to see the retreating figure of the large woman, swinging her hips, off to some isolated spot to be alone.

They share a breakfast of scrambled eggs, hearty bacon strips, and guava juice.

"Listen to this." Louis reads from the spare local newspaper: "'Chris Johnson, age 13, was found at the Emerald Pool yesterday, after a long hunt by authorities. Mr. Johnson ran away from his home in Connecticut, USA, where he had read about Dominica in his school library. Before getting on a plane to return home he told reporters he loved the island and hoped to return.' Wow, long way to run away from home."

"I always wanted to run away when I was little," Jill reflects, stirring her coffee and peering into the shallow cup. "But I never had the guts. Somehow, I knew my parents would find me and bring me home, and I'd be in worse shape than before."

"Your mind overpowered you then, too? I ran away once, to a friend's house—Jimmy Black. I still remember his name. He had a huge dirt hill in his backyard for motorbiking. I guess my parents were called right away. They told the Blacks to go along. I was given so many chores, I never had time to ride the bike, so I decided I'd rather go back home."

Jill gives an absent smile, finishes the sweet juice.

Her husband snaps the newspaper shut. "I'm going to the fort today, sans guide. You want to come?" he asks warily.

"Yes." She tries to look nonchalant, stands up slowly, hoping to erase eagerness from her movements.

Sun pushes through the clouds, highlighting the mist that spins around them, giving them a brief glimpse of "liquid sunshine," making Jill feel almost happy to be there, on the green island of Wai'tikubuli. Louis opens her car door in a gesture reminiscent of their dating days. She slides over and unlocks his door.

Fort Shirly is a partial ruin, one of the few monuments left to reveal the inevitable colonization. Jill feels the bold convictions of the French soldiers and the displaced ideals oozing from the dark, damp stones of the fort. After the long climb up through the dense woods, scented with honeysuckle and fermented leaves, she separates from Louis, leaving him gazing over a parapet, finds her own way to the battle room. The thick walls and a need for protection allowed for only narrow, paneless windows cut high into the granite. She sees a soldier leaning into its tunnel, aiming, that small view perhaps his last sight on earth.

The lizards wouldn't care. When she stands still, breathing her only movement, they hurry across the sun-baked dust outside, dart out from the shadows and into the light that only penetrates a few feet, then change skin color to match their new place. If only people could do that, she thinks. Walk into, or out of, a situation and be able to adapt instantly, to become part of the new situation completely.

Louis rounds the doorway. "Ready to eat? There's a great view from the wall out front."

The low fortress wall meanders without purpose up the hill to the fortress and beyond. It is too low for defense, simply a statement of boundaries. Lichen scratches her bare thighs. Louis pulls out homemade flat sugar cookies, *kenapes*, and oranges (small greenish things) from a brown paper bag.

"I can't believe we're the only ones here. It's like we're the only tourists on this island," Louis says.

"I know. Kind of nice, though. No lines, no garbage, no loud Americans to embarrass us."

They watch fishermen in the bay check their traps. The Technicolor-blue ocean seems very far away.

Jill bites into the skin of a *kenape* to crack it, discards it for the perfect round peachlike fruit inside. "We should go snorkeling."

A man vaults the stone wall and lands next to her, as if dropped from the sky; another man lands on Louis's right. Peripherally, she sees a man appear on the fortress above them, and sudden instinct senses a fourth lurking behind, in the fort's shadows.

A holster hangs over the shoulder of the small, muscled man, almost touching her. With startling clarity she thinks, This is it. *This is it.*

The young man caresses the holster with his right hand. A black gun handle shows. His left hand is missing.

Danger pounds in her ears. She is surrounded by it. But something takes over. A sort of calm. Maybe it comes from Louis, who begins talking in a level voice.

"Hi. We're from the U.S. Beautiful island you have here."

Jill knows they are being sized up. In the next few seconds, a major decision will be made. She senses by the man at her side.

She makes her own. She picks up the bag of *kenapes* and hands them to him. "Would you like some?"

She's bought them time. He takes a fistful of his island fruit, bites savagely, chews and spits the pits out on the grass. She watches the end of his arm, the stump, skin folded in like the end of a roll of cookie dough, tough but vulnerable.

Louis continues talking in measured tones. Jill can't listen, her senses are too attuned to the process of eating *kenapes*. She feels an unspoken dialogue between her and the man eating with one hand. He stares straight ahead, as she does, at the ocean's expanse, but they are really speaking to each other, wild rivals foraging with their ears pricked and alert. *Don't you dare. I should, I must, you don't need it.*

Louis's hand creeps over hers, his only concession to danger.

Some other, silent signal shoots between the two men on the wall. They hop off and disappear as quickly as they came.

"Let's get the hell out of here." Louis pulls her back over the wall. They leave the lunch behind and half run back down through the woods, still alert to every sound and crackle. At the empty parking lot, Jill's heart begins to slow. But she continues to clutch Louis's hand as the rush of adrenaline makes her sick, so much so that she leans over and retches onto the hot asphalt.

"Hi, Mom." Jill tries to calm her voice, hears the shakes in it.

"Why do you always call when I'm watching *Mystery*?"

"Are you eating?"

"No, I'm done. I had the meatloaf tonight. It was good. Why didn't you call yesterday?"

"I just wanted to say hi, Mom, I should really get going."

Click. The dial tone comes on. Jill stares at the receiver for a moment. Louis comes out of the bathroom in jeans, toweling dry his blond hair. They have decided to stay the final twenty-four hours they have left, and reported the men to the authorities, where they got pointed stares at their wedding rings and watches. She looks on now as he steps into his sneakers, always the left one first. He picks out a T-shirt from the suitcase, tosses it over his head. She knows he will now comb his hair, four strokes, and look for his wallet. She marvels at the fact that he is still there, with her, in the same room, even after all her rejection.

On their final day, Louis bends to her wish to go snorkeling. Leaving their jewelry in the hotel safe, they discover the dive centers are closed for another month, but are sent to a hotel willing to rent them flippers, masks, and snorkels for five U.S. dollars. Two local boys offer to take them to Champagne Springs. The hotel assures them that the boys, in their faded shorts, are professional divers, completely safe to go out with.

The sea is calm, and Jill is glad to finally be in it. The outboard skims the top, slowing when they reach the landmark that guides them off of Soufriere.

"I go with you and show you around," the older boy says, putting on his mask. Jill takes her shirt off, revealing her bikini top, but leaves her shorts on for modesty. They pull on their flippers, spit in their masks, rinse them in the saltwater, then put them on and fall backward into the Caribbean.

Immediately Jill feels at home in this other world. Sea fans and anemones wave in underwater currents, coral grows in bunches as haphazardly as trees grow in forests above. In the boat the boy had explained that the sealife was recovering from overfishing and toxic fertilizers that once washed down from the steep mountain farms into the ocean. Briefly she thought of Ron, who seemed so far in her past, a small snapshot of an experience, superfluous now.

The guide points out a striped yellow fish, then gestures at them to follow.

Up ahead they see sparkling lights. She kicks more rapidly to get to the underwater freshwater springs. Warm air bubbles up like carbonation, and Jill does feel like she's in the middle of a large champagne glass, little round pockets of pink light sailing to the surface, tickling her limbs as they pass. She lets herself float, facing Louis, luxuriating in the light and warmth and the sound of her own, hard breathing. She pushes the breath from her lungs and dives deeper, until she's at the center looking up at the white sun. Louis touches her and thumbs up.

At the surface, he gasps, "I'm going back to the boat. I'm getting seasick from the waves."

"Are you OK?"

"Yeah. I just need out."

"Should we leave?"

"No, you stay as long as you want. It's beautiful down there. Where are you gonna get a chance to swim in champagne again?"

She watches him make his way back to where the other boy waits patiently. The guide surfaces and she explains.

"I will take you further down the ledge."

She follows him, not ready to give up this underworld. She watches him dive deeper than she can go, and detach something from a rock. She is losing breath and resurfaces, and he brings it to her, a sea horse, built for stability rather than speed, as big as her middle finger, rock-colored with a layer of algae covering it. She takes it from him gingerly, surprised at how soft and fat its belly is. She is used to seeing them as dehydrated souvenirs. And then she realizes she is probably holding a pregnant male. The male is the homebody, she knows, clinging tightly to a turbulent foundation, taking its role in stride, accepting the mate it has bonded to for the season as she visits him each day. The eyes appear closed, trusting and calm. The tail searches for a place to anchor while she holds it.

She cries, her tears collecting in the mask. Am I the only one who's ever cried under water? she asks herself, and hands the creature back. He returns it to its seaweed base; she calms her breathing, and follows him down.

Jill sees and feels the light change. Darkness is developing above and below. She rocks more solidly in the water. Surfacing and riding the choppy waves, she sees a large black cloud approaching from the south, seeming to rise out of the distant black water itself. The fuzzy outline is spreading quickly, pushing the water and the wind before it.

The diver tells her not to worry, it's not a bad storm. To her, it looks like angry gods. She can tell he's eager to go back down to the world he loves, and does so without her. The cloud arrives overhead and rains down, and still she rocks on the surface, looking to Louis in the boat. The guide behind her continues to dive, content to wait out the storm. The boat's passengers look resigned to wait it out, too. But she can't bear to see Louis's back bent so long under the cold rain, waiting. She begins a determined crawl through weather-churned waters, wondering how love can be so different and so subtle, so hard to recognize and accept.

GHOST DANCE

He didn't know them right away; it was a year before he began to even sense they were there—a cold draught, a murmur, a sharp change in the air like nuggets being dropped on metal scales.

And after two years on the southern Montana prairie, along the snaking Southern River with banks overwhelmed with discarded rocks, signs of earlier plunder, a river that still yielded gold dust, Brandy knew for sure he wasn't alone. The draughts became visions, the murmurs became voices, and the changes in the air now carried sound.

You could say the sole caretaker of the restored mining town along this river was now haunted. But during the hours of 10 a.m. to 3 p.m., Monday to Saturday, June to September, he was surrounded by the living—like Prissy, who ran the front desk, selling tickets to tourists passing by on Highway 1. Ageless, with a gray-white bristly mustache, a biker boyfriend, and a sweet, chirping voice, she reminded him of the frontierswomen who had settled Montana—she'd look just right in a bonnet and long dress, swinging an axe to cut wood for the cook stove.

Prissy mothered him, checked up on him during the long winter months. She'd snowshoe over high drifts, bearing a stew or a goose thawed and roasted from the fall hunt. "Hellooo," her voice would ring out, breaking winter's silence. "Glad you're still alive. Here's some dinner. Should last you a week." He'd take the enamel kettle from her mittened hands and ask her in, desperate for company. Her food wasn't fancy, just good and hardy.

The town had been brought back to life by his boss, Wilson Whiteman, a local logger with a vision borne from peering through the dust-encrusted pane of one of the few buildings still standing, facing the highway. He was surprised to see flowered Victorian wallpaper still intact, though dripping with water stains, and a puffy couch and matching chair. No one had looted in all these years. The idea came to him that people would pay money to see a real ghostown. Many abandoned pioneer homesteads and shanties littered the prairie. For the price of carting them over and laying them down, he could restore the original town plot.

Once the job was complete, Wilson needed a full-time caretaker. Brandy saw the ad in the Calvin *Pennysaver* and applied. He had nowhere to live, and he had nothing. His construction company had gone bankrupt; his childless marriage had ended the second he realized his wife was never coming back from girls' night out. (They divorced several months later.) Free room and board and a chance to do what he loved best—building and repairing—was perfect.

He was given a log cabin, found nearby, built with more enthusiasm than materials by some rancher's grandfather. It faced the post office, saloon, other cabins and one-room lean-tos. The schoolhouse steeple rose above them all, piercing the distant mountain range. "Do what you want to the inside, but leave the outside authentic," Wilson instructed.

A new roof, coat of plaster, toilet behind a screen, a stove and refrigerator, and he was home.

When the town was filled with tourists and filmmakers, Brandy retreated to his cabin, away from the lookers poking and actors shooting blanks around the town he now considered to be his. He kept curtains drawn against curious eyes, and napped or whittled. After the last tourist left he locked the entrance gates and made sure all museum doors were closed to protect the interiors from weather and animals. Sometimes Prissy followed him, sweeping dust and leaves that onlookers had dragged in. Prissy was the last person he'd see, and he'd wave as she hopped onto the back of her boyfriend Zack's motorbike and rode away.

The town lay before him. Still with daylight left, he would roam the dirt streets and wooden boardwalks. He hopped the acrylic barriers that kept tourists from entering too far into the store or house. He tried on hats, poked around in old tobacco containers and pipes, continued the game of solitaire left unfinished on the saloon table. On nights when his cabin walls threatened to close in, he'd take his dinner of scrambled eggs or stew to the fancy house and eat at a mahogany table set for twelve, over which hung a working chandelier, or to one of the cabins and eat at a wooden table set with a humble bread board and pewter pitcher. He grew accustomed to the old portrait photographs that watched him eating by warm lamplight. Every sound was amplified—the crickets, the grouse drumming its wings, the prairie wolf howling, his fork against the plate.

It was on one of those nights, eating dinner in the cabin next to his own, when he heard a noise behind him. It was a noise he couldn't place—and he'd grown so familiar with all of them. It was like silk against silk. He turned but saw nothing in the evening's August melon light. And after that night, he began to hear more—footsteps, harnesses clanking—and he felt more—draughts, as if a door was opening, pushing air into the room.

He got scared. He bought a hound and kept it tethered up outside his cabin. But what he was really scared of was himself.

He spoke to no one of this, convinced it was the desolation of the place, no phone in his cabin, snowcapped mountains always seeming so far away and out of his reach. But he couldn't leave, knowing he had a place there. So he started to ask people over for dinner or a beer. It helped. For a time, Prissy and Zack's energy filled the place and left no room for the sounds. Roy and Ken, the plumbers, kept him laughing with their stories about Wilson, the bossman, daring him to forget his troubles. And Wilson himself, because he was the builder, reminded him that the place was manmade. They pulled him back to their world for a while.

After an uneventful winter, he welcomed the spring and the task of patching sod roofs. A dry summer followed. June, usually so wet, saw only sporadic rainfall. In July, when the sun beat down, punishing the grass and trees, he'd walk around the perimeter of the town looking and sniffing for the beginnings of brush fire. One day, dripping sweat all the way to the soles of his feet, finding himself a little faint, he sat down under the post office's cool overhang. He knew if he sat quiet long enough, the prairie would come to life. He watched young prairie dogs dart from hiding—from behind rocks, mounds, wagon wheels—to play in the road dust. A hawk circled overhead. The robin that nested over his doorway now kept an eye on her new, speckle-bellied brood pecking in the grass. A chipmunk found the peach pit he'd intentionally left on a boulder and turned it over in its small paws, examining. Silk rubbed against silk.

He snapped his head to the right. He swore he heard his name, whispered as softly as the silk sounded. It drew him to his feet, down the steps, down the main street to the schoolhouse, one of the original buildings that had survived one hundred years of prairie weather. The front door was open like an invitation. He walked past wooden school desks, a teacher's podium, a silhouette of Lincoln, to the open doorway of the rear room. She lay on the schoolteacher's rope bed, in a white cotton shift, crying. He moved to comfort her instinctively, and she dissolved.

"Do you know anything about the schoolteacher who lived here?" he asked Wilson.

Wilson shrugged. "All we know is her name was Miz Annabelle

Fourier, age twenty-two, French. She's on record for filing a complaint, charging two men in town with assault. Far as I can tell, charges were dropped. Why you wanna know?"

"I just want to get to know the place better."

The prairie comes to life in the quiet. To Brandy, the other ghosts remained sounds and stirrings only. Why only Annabelle showed herself, he'd never know. Maybe he'd conjured her, maybe he'd brought her back from the dead the way the Indians had hoped to bring back their slaughtered ancestors. And it was his one regret that she never spoke to him. He heard other voices, but not hers. He thought maybe it took so much effort for her to become visible that she had to give up her voice, like the fairy tale mermaid. But after a few months of brief appearances she became ever present— in his cabin, in the haberdashery, in the tall grass by the low river. When her school bell rang out, the rope pulled by a tourist, the reverberations rolled through him. She was not beautiful, his ghost, but he loved her freckled face, strong forearms, wispy red hair, and penetrating eyes that forced him to care. They tied him to that place, those eyes, fed him and kept him steady.

Brandy let the faucet water run over his comb, then ran it through his hair, carefully matting down the strands on top, now baby-fine. The music hall beckoned him, the velvet dark night alive with chirps and umpahs and tinny musical notes as the large organs ran their course. Clowns' heads twisted and turned, ballerinas pirouetted, and horses galloped round. In the midst of this old glory, Annabelle met him in her best watered silk gown, her hair, in ringlets, copper under the overhead lights.

"Will you dance, Miz Annie?" He bowed low in his jeans and boots. She smiled and moved as close as two different centuries could get without destroying the other's illusion. And every sense in the one alive vibrated with sound and rapture.

THE DARK SUN

—

April

We move in during the time when the monarch butterflies emigrate from Mexico to Canada. It is through a light curtain of orange-powdered wings that I first see my new home, the bushes, driveway, rooftop alive with fluttering movement. And it is with a feeling of foreboding that we drive slowly up to the garage, unable to keep from crushing some of the sweet insects. They are prepared to escape predators with their erratic flight, but they have no protection against human inventions, and as I alight from the car, their dusty wings caress my cheek and hair, and I try not to look at the wheels of the car that has driven us over 2,000 miles. Lee did not tell me how featureless this land is, how unwelcoming the sun is, how so much expires as it passes through.

Such strange things grow here, so different from the delicate, almost puritan-like flowers in the east. I'm used to paper-petaled poppies; flax petals that fall in the lightest breeze; baby's breath, an enormous lacy cloud made up of tiny clouds. Here, the brightness and heavy perfumes assail my senses. Bougainvillea chokes the house, portulaca's fleshy branches spread like a weed along the driveway, and the pepper bushes, harmless now, will be a hazard to the baby. Even the trees are something to adjust to. I see miserable palm trees, dry, flaky, peeling, fringed; not stately, smooth, and generous in their protective shade. We have a Yupon holly. Lee tends to it. According to the local nursery it is infested with fourteen different kinds of bugs. I watch him from the window as he goes out, bundled for safety, and sprays the bush with something that is illegal. I did not want him to endanger us in this way, but he insists. So I watch him bend and pick and peer at the fourteen varieties. He caresses the dying leaves and gazes for a time at the whole sad thing growing less dense every day. I say let the damn bush die of natural causes—try to save us.

Letters and phone calls are my lifeline to the past, a past that now seems prehistoric in its distance from my present life. I have only been in the Rio Grand Valley for several weeks, but it's enough to see what a mistake I made. I feel lured here by Lee with promises of a Better Standard of Living, that B.S.O.L. equation that is as good as a steel trap. I hire Lolita as a maid, to cook and clean. We are lucky—she speaks English well. Still, it is unsettling to have a stranger handling our personal things, living as part of our household. But this gives me time to write, and she will be a big help when the baby comes. Things look good on the outside, but inside they are rotting. I am reminded of a man I once saw in the New York subway. He looked Peruvian, like he should have been wearing a poncho and broad-brimmed straw hat. Instead he was sunk into Western clothes, with a comb in his back pocket. His chest was concave, his eyes downcast. He sat on the plastic seat as if afraid to rest his full weight on it—he clung to the metal bar. Only once did he look up, catching me studying him. His eyes were a shock—two perfect circles of fear. I have never seen such round, frightened eyes. Before he left the train he glanced back at me. I wondered then what our connection was. How could he have known?

May

Gilberto is just down the road. Yet I can't bring myself to venture out, so vulnerable have I become, so sensitive to men's gazes. Lolita says it will be good for the baby. Chili. He is a barber who cuts, trims, shaves, scolds, and advises and stirs the best chili in the Valley. When we drive by, I search into his house of four walls, try to pierce the sharp slants of light that interrupt the darkness beyond windows holding no glass. Lee drives by so quickly there is not enough time to discover whatever it is I am trying to find. Afternoons and evenings a few local men squat in the pebbled dust outside his shop, waiting their turn. I ask Lolita to get the chili for me. She is brave in some ways, and one of them. She can walk by their curiously penetrating gazes, up into Gilberto's house, and back again with a pot of his fiery beans. No, I say, I will only go halfway, then turn back. I know I need the exercise.

I read this in the paper today: "Lady Who Slept in a Mercedes" is the headline. A woman drove up in front of a man's house in Corona del Mar. He watched her from his window as she alighted from the shiny vehicle and with white-gloved hands draped the car in a cover, dipped under it, and stayed there for the night. I imagine the man rose early next morning, eager to see if there were any new developments in the puzzle. His curiosity was not assuaged—when he looked out again across a lawn in early morning, she was already packing away the car cover and driving off. Who was she, I ask, that did what so many women want to do? Just get in the car, and drive; drive to another place, another spot, with clean gloves and a clean car, no mess, no bother, no one in pursuit, a clean getaway. But to where? I wish I could find her, wish I could ask what she found, if the place she rests at is enough for forever, or just for another night. If she left anyone behind, and most important, what was the final act that sent her off.

I force myself to leave the house today, to go to the doctor. I look at the gestation chart and what is inside me, realize that it has gone from reptilian to human. I am afraid for it now, want to protect it. The doctor says not to worry, that my cervix might need to be sewn closed, but that everything is under control. Am I? I wonder.

Am I capable of keeping this all together? Will the scream I feel sometimes moving up my throat, like mercury moves up a thermometer, explode and send my baby from me like a shooting star? I leave the office, trying to keep calm, breathing deeply. I pass a drugstore on the way home, and pull in. It is something familiar, a tie to home. The aisles are orderly, the products alphabetical by brand name, so that whatever I want is easy to find. My breathing returns to normal as I poke at the small samples. Can I help you? A voice startles me. I pull my finger away from the display, as if guilty of stealing. N-no, I stammer, Just looking. I realize this sounds crazy—who just browses in a drugstore? But the man smiles and leaves me. He is dark, beautiful.

My mother calls. We are suddenly on a new level, finally adults; we can talk about this experience as equals, not just as mother and daughter. Even marriage can't be talked about equally because the situations are so different. But not this. She tells me to rub olive oil on my nipples to prepare them for nursing and not to listen to other people's horror stories. They love to tell pregnant women horror stories about their own births or somebody else's, she says. I start to cry. What's wrong? she asks. Nothing, I say. For the first time in my life. As a daughter I have always shared everything with my mother, from the first discoveries of pebbles and insects to the decisions of contraception. But I cannot bring myself to tell her I'm lonely, that my husband is doing what the magazines say at least 50 percent of all husbands will do, that I'm scared every day that the worst horror story here—that someone could give my child the evil eye—could happen, thus deforming the one thing that must be perfect. Because nothing else is. I don't tell her all this because she cannot understand, and might ask me to come home, to give up.

Every morning Lee leaves with the darkness, kisses me twice— once on my cheek, once on my stomach. I wonder how he can keep up this charade, this performance of chaste husband and father-to-be. Yet still I pray that he returns safely from across the border. I imagine him hit by one of their yellow buses, bleeding by the side of the road, no one stopping to help a gringo. Maybe an ambulance will show up in an hour to collect his drained body. And I pray hard to whomever, whatever will listen that he is not falsely arrested by border police. He is all I have, all that separates me from "out there" until the baby arrives. And I try to keep images of entwining and knotted male and female limbs at bay.

The Yupon holly is dead. We haven't decided if we will replace it yet.

I can't even bring myself to go food shopping any longer. The idea of even setting forth, outside, starting my Jeep and heading for the Circle K . . . the glowing sky . . . flat fields . . . abandoned housing projects. . . . The very thought of the boys who eagerly pack the brown bags into the car . . . so extravagant with their smiles, accepting no tips, their joy in working transparent through their cocoa coloring. . . . Is she that color, too? I shake even as my hand considers closing around the doorknob and twisting. If I step further than the stairs, anxiety washes down like icy drops calculated to make me shiver and quake. The mailbox is a challenge. At least I can get to it and return without fear of fainting, though I feel neighbors' eyes, like rodents jumbled together in a sleeping heap, peering, half-lidded, from beneath blinds and shades. So poor Lolita goes for me. I say poor Lolita because yesterday she told me, while chopping onions, that she comes from Chihuahua. Her father worked on a ranch, and while he worked the cattle and her mother took care of her brothers and sisters, Lolita wandered. Her favorite place she nicknamed *El Trono del Rey*, the King's Throne, a towering rock formation. One day, tired of playing around in its shadow, she climbed to the top. It was the highest point to the horizon, close to the sun, everything so small below—the cattle, the buildings—and she felt like a king for that day—good, strong, invincible I think she was trying to say. The mountain lions playing in the sun on the warm rocks below her were her subjects. But the feeling disappeared when she returned to the ground, and it was then she decided to leave her country where she could only feel small, and go to the United States of America, where she could live like a king. Poor Lolita, chopping onions. We are much the same. She is away from her roots, surrounded by her own people, Mexican Americans, who reject her. I am away from where I am Joan. Who is Joan now, I wonder, when everything defining and framing is removed? My whiteness is a torch that blinds the people on the border, and this image of me that they gather into their eyes is reflected back on me.

For Lolita's birthday, I get up at 5 a.m. (she rises at 6) and fix her breakfast. This is not hard to do as the baby is keeping me up at night, kicking and turning. I fix her fried eggs on toast with salsa sauce on top, put it on my wedding china, squeeze orange juice into a crystal glass, and place the paper crown I made in the tray's center. She is surprised when I knock and enter, modestly clutches her gown at the neck as if I were a man. We have not seen each other in such an intimate way. How vulnerable she looks without makeup, how pointy her breasts are without a padded bra. I place the tray on her bed. Happy Birthday, Lolita, I say, You are king today, and I am your servant. She frowns slightly when I place the crown on her head, looks offended. But I persist: I'll cook and clean today, you take a break and go out. No, I'll stay here and work, she says, poking at the crown as women used to poke at bobby pins. That's ridiculous, I laugh, Don't be a martyr. Her eyes fall, and I am looking at her black lashes. Nowhere to go, she mumbles, and begins to shake. I know about these tremors. I reach out and hold her, so she knows there is something solid to rest on, at least for the moment. Tomorrow, I am sure, we will act as if we have forgotten.

I read that a man in Gonzales has adopted an underweight lion. The photograph shows the rancher cradling the lion's oversized head in his arms—the lion looks thin, but at peace. Some ranchers buy lions to make a sport of hunting them, but this rancher is attached—I can see the bond, even in black and white. I think of the unlikely friendship, how the victim can save the predator.

June

It is my birthday, and Lolita wants to return the favor. I am not feeling well lately. The doctor says it's nothing to worry about, just to rest. Lee leaves a package on the nightstand—a new watch, with numerals. He knows I can't read time without them. No card, no message. Lolita takes the watch off my wrist and then helps me to take off my gown and underpants. I lie naked and swollen beneath her casual gaze. She props me on my side and I smell the immediate scent of coconut as she opens the bottle. Her hands are warm and wet as she massages my body, sliding, gliding, kneading. This is the first time in months that my body has been touched like this. How important just to be touched, I think, as she moves to my front and massages my legs, arms, neck, chest. My nipples harden but I am unashamed and she continues down to my hard stomach. The baby kicks and she stops to feel, and I press a hand over hers for a second. She continues down to my pelvic area, skitters her hand across my thighs. When it's over she slips the sheet over me, covers the oil and leaves the room with a whisper of sound. The ceiling fan overhead begins to turn—she's thought of everything. As my body cools, I look at Lee's picture. He looks back, hands stuffed in his pockets, shirt unbuttoned at the collar, receding hairline and rugged complexion. I wanted it to be you, I say, Did you want it to be me when you touched your girl? I think of Lolita and realize she knows about Lee, too. That what she did for me took as much effort as the hug I gave her took for me. That her circle is much smaller and a hug is nothing to give, but this is more. The baby is peaceful inside. It, too, is learning to relax.

The sweet potatoes are being attacked by white fly this year. The fly sucks the life from the plant and leaves a "honeydew" film behind. At night, dogs bark at howling coyotes. Special places to obtain bail bonds line the highway, one after another. Texans cruise U.S. Highway

83 in their custom-built trucks, or *choo-choos*, cruise by churches offering to sell a ticket to fly to heaven. On weekends it takes about two hours by car to cross the border into Mexico, so people walk instead for miles. Or you can stay at the Hotel Amigo, close to the border, with people, mostly Mexican Americans from up north, spending the night before the long trip home, with a car loaded down with whatever booty they could get through the border police. There is better shopping in Reynosa. From the other side, men drown in the Rio Grande, poor swimmers trying to reach the polluted U.S. shore. And through all this the cotton grows, bolls willing, strong and high, far and wide, covering the turned brown soil like snow. I forced myself to stop the Jeep yesterday, to get out and pick a piece of cotton. It was so eerie and almost wonderful to feel, just as it feels in the plastic bag, round and soft but for the prickly burrs. And picking it, I dare to say, I got a better sense than I ever had before of the back-breaking, finger-punishing task it must have been to reap these snowy fields under this hellish sun; then to go "home," watched by unfriendly eyes. I am beginning to learn. The cotton on my dresser is a reminder.

I find reasons to go to the drugstore. Vitamins, sanitary needs, shaving gel, anything to get away from my situation and see this man. He recognizes me now, addresses me with a warm smile and calls me Mrs. Colyer. I don't feel a barrier against my whiteness. He leans over the counter and chats. Soon I discover he is married and has two children. This is fine with me. I envy his wife from a distance, and his domestic life, so neat and uncomplicated from the outside. When the Texas dust blows hard and strong and leaves me sneezing and with watery eyes, unable to sit on my patio, he recommends a painter's mask. Here, he says (demonstrating how to put it on), I have to wear one when I mow the lawn—it filters out the dust particles and pollen. The blue material is bright against his shiny brown skin. I would buy anything at this point to have something in common with him.

Lee wants me to go to his company picnic. When I first learned of TRW's annual outside party, I looked forward to it. A chance to meet new people, to see Mexico. Now I dread it. Coco will be there, of course, and the thought makes me ill. Literally. Now I will be able to put a face on the headless body I imagine wrapped around Lee. It will be much worse to know the face of this monstrosity that haunts me and twists me up inside, to know who writes those simple misspelled notes to my husband on tacky Hallmark cards. Much better to be a ghost of the imagination. I am growing so superstitious here; I try not to think of these thoughts, afraid they might twist the baby. Lolita says the women will be in dresses, even gowns. They take great pride in their appearance. I look at myself in the dresser mirror, see a pale wan face, pale hair, falling in loose strands from its tie. I am sad and happy and angry I am so obviously pregnant—I am sad that my figure won't compete; I am happy to show her what she probably doesn't know; I am angry that society makes me think I am ugly like this. Suddenly, I remember the life I was trying to escape, marriage to Lee the only way I could gain freedom to write. This is what I escaped to? I laugh and cry at the irony.

It is going to be one hundred degrees, Lee says, Don't wear a dress, that's ridiculous. So I don a T-shirt, cotton pants and sandals, sunscreen, a cap with a visor, and sunglasses. You can't go anywhere here without sunglasses—the sun burns your eyes. It takes all the strength I can call up to climb into the hot car. I'm in hell. Burning up, frying. The road ahead is even worse than the road behind. We travel silently down Route 2. My senses are sharp. The air conditioner roars, the car's metal grinds, the air shrieks through the vents. Lee is nervous—his wedding ring keeps time against the steering wheel to his own inner rhythm. I turn on the radio to Travis Tritt singing about getting rid of a woman for the price of a quarter. How easy for him. It is Saturday and we left early to avoid the traffic crossing the border, but there is still a line. Soon we are through and across the Rio Grande. Welcome to Mexico, Lee says, I'm going to take you through the worst parts. We drive through Reynosa's winding streets, stopping at signs reading ALTO. Hotels, shops, restaurants, roadside stands. We reach a highway and Mexico stands before us, unobstructed, vulnerable, abused. The land is flat and featureless, polluted, gray, depressed. I string so many adjectives together because so many are needed to describe what most never see. It is not what I expected—no lushness or brightness, no place for a Club Med. I could never have imagined such poverty. Rows of lean-tos, shacks and huts, stretching beyond view, surrounded by swamps and holes filled with garbage and sewage. Parts of cars, Dali-like, strew the surreal scape. My hands go protectively over my stomach, as if to shield my child's view. And what is even more of a shock is how clean and bright and happy Lee's Mexican co-workers are. Lolita is right. The women are dressed in bright ruffled dresses of all lengths. They dance and hold their children under the shade of the tikki huts, looking cool and content. I am a curiosity, as I am everywhere, but they are respectful of the boss's wife. I had expected sympathetic or laughing glances, but instead they are shy and warm. They gesture to my stomach and nod, approving. I nod back. They offer to let me hold their children. Miguel proudly shows his six-month-old baby girl, his eighth child. She looks up at me, her slippery mouth a sweet pout. I can't help but kiss her rosy cheek, and Miguel smiles. Lee is drinking beer and keeping a watchful lookout. The DJ plays loud Mexican rock music. Through all this I also keep an eye out. But no one introduces an exotic beauty named Coco. By midmorning I learn that she is not coming. I am both relieved and disappointed. After finishing a meal of potato salad (I leave the fajitas and refried beans untouched), I remove myself from the activity. I need to find the bathroom. After relieving myself in an open restroom, I gather courage to wander around the park— I need to get rid of the adrenaline. The caretakers live on the park's land, in two *jascales.* They sit outside and watch the party, watch me approach. I take a deep breath and smile, uncertain of their reception. *Hola,* I say, using what little Spanish I have picked up, and, *Bonitas,* gesturing to what must be the daughters of an older woman. This breaks their hard stares. The woman lets me pet their baby goat. I wonder if it is to be raised for milk or meat. I decide milk is probably more valuable. I feel less shaky, as if I have a place amongst these girls lounging on old couches and benches. I have a connection to this woman and her progeny, by the simple fact that I, too, am a woman, soon to give birth. I kneel and pet the goat at the woman's feet, rubbing the bristly fur, as if for luck. Maybe we can get a goat for the baby.

You should go, Lolita says, the ceramic bowl she places in front of me heavy with emphasis and spiciness. I choke for a moment on the oily steam. How can I eat this? I ask her, I can't even smell it! Don't worry, she says, That feeling won't stay; eat—it's good for the *bebé*. He will bounce with delight, and it will make him grow strong legs. Strong legs are good—they take men far. She spoons a bit of chili to my lips. Reluctantly I hold my breath and flick my tongue to it, cautiously, wary of being burned. The touch is not enough so I take the spoon into my mouth, closing down. Heat registers first, then delight as the spices infuse what I imagine to be my forehead. And I picture them traveling down through my body, through the cord, to the surprised being at the other end. And I imagine it swimming furiously for more. You should go, she says again, Gilberto will only be there until the month's end. He is being kicked off for more crop land. The house will come down and next year we will see cotton. So go, *sí*? He will like it. I reluctantly agree to go before he leaves, at a time when no one is there but Gilberto, starting up the cauldron fire.

July

Lolita's manner is skittish and watchful, absent. I ask her what is it that is making her so nervous? She tells me the "dark sun" is coming. She explains that on Thursday, the moon will cross in front of the sun, and that in Mexico some believe the world might come to an end. I don't believe this, she says, But it is a bad thing. Sick people get sicker, old people die, and . . . I can see her eyeing my stomach. I am suddenly shaking her shoulders. And what, Lolita? What else? She walks to the sink and begins rinsing breakfast dishes. But she

knows she must answer. I know someone, she whispers through
running water, whose baby was born on an eclipse. It was dead,
and had only one side of its face. That's ridiculous, I bark,
Superstition! You should know better than that! She turns from
the sink and her eyes are wide. No, she insists, This is true. You
must not leave the house that day. Stay inside, *señora,* and wear
something metal. It will absorb the sun's rays. The rest of the
afternoon I sit writing in my living room. The furniture is all new,
purchased in the Valley—white, pure, clean against a neutral beige
background. And I look out at the pool, lined with Mexican tiles,
and beyond that to the flat cotton fields, waves of white under the
hot sun. How can this feeling of dread exist in me, in such an
ordered environment? Is there no way to tame it, to rub out that
instinctual fear? For I am, in spite of myself, a little fearful, and
turn from my stagnant writing to put on the news.

I wait for this dark sun to come. Lee leaves for work as usual. He
won't stay home, says I'm becoming paranoid. Of course I can't
tell him about the safety pin Lolita pinned to my bra to ward off
goodness knows what. We draw the blinds against the early morning
sun, and wait. And it seems to me that this is what I have been
doing all my life—waiting in trepidation for my life to unfold,
expecting it to be all disaster. There are *quinceañeras* here, girls who
are dressed in wedding gowns at the age of fifteen and "married"
to the church—a sort of confirmation. I believe these girls are
married twice. Once to idealism, purity, hope. A second time to
reality and hard facts. In my culture women are only to marry once—
so that idealism and reality are inextricably intertwined in a war,
and we constantly battle within ourselves against the two. Men are
not the only ones with split iconic images of the opposite sex—
women split savior and child. And we wait. What happens when
we grow tired of waiting? I wonder, as I sense the light outside
beginning to change. It is a subtle shift. Lolita stops vacuuming and
comes to sit beside me. She won't let me look outside at first, but
when I insist, saying that the blinds are metal, she allows me to pull

down a slat. Outside, the world is changed. The trees, grass, water, sky, all look other-worldly. It is not my world right now. It is glazed over by a pinkish-yellow light that remains for about fifteen minutes. Birds flit under it before roosting, skittish as Lolita. They look out of their element, fish in an aquarium lit by an unnatural light. The fig tree outside shivers.

We hear on the news that the vendors in the Hildago Street market have closed down for the day. The busy streets are silent, full of strange shadows and light. A few palace workers and citizens are braver than most, but still stick to the darkened areas. Rumors run rampant, fears are real and imagined. Parents keep their children at home, afraid they might peer at the eclipse and be blinded. Manufactured sunglasses aren't enough protection. I am educated, I tell myself, I know this is all wrong. Yet sitting next to Lolita, nervously tapping her lemonade glass, I am very aware that there shouldn't even be this question in my mind.

The eclipse fades, the sunlight is real again. Lee comes home from work, restoring normalcy. He shakes his head and complains that many of his workers didn't show up. You are eating *cocido,* I tell him, Lolita showed me how to make it. She says they make it in big cauldrons on her ranch. He looks down blankly at the stew of beef, carrots, onions, and potatoes. I made it for you, I add, testing. I thought you hated Mexican food? Well, I answer, I'm beginning to get used to it. Good, he smiles, and I see the dimples that used to bring that welcome, aching feeling to my chest, and I find that they still can. Good, thank you, and he spears a section of meat with his fork and sends it to his mouth with a flourish. How's your writing? he asks, for the first time in months. I tell him about the poem I've been struggling with, trying to make the language fit the emotion. He looks at me, and he knows I am trying.

I am beginning to see beauty here. It's in the hummingbird I saw propelling itself through the purple vines. It's in this space, this elbow room, which at first closed in on me, accentuating my aloneness. Now I feel larger, wider, more in proper perspective. (Or is it just the *bebé*?) No, it is this vast sky covering the landscape like a bowl, like the planetariums I visited as a child. And you can watch the heavens move, change, shake, flare, not like you can in the east. I want my child to grow up under such a sky, to be reminded daily of the universe. But the people are what have really changed things for me—Lolita with her dreams and care, and the owner of the drugstore who I can't, who I won't, ever touch, who has touched me. Maybe this is what Lee sees in Coco. Maybe if we stay here long enough, we'll absorb some of the smells, colors, sweetness of the surroundings and become more worthy of each other. Maybe.

I try to ignore the ghosts of customers, apparitions staring me down as they do everywhere I go, though I am growing accustomed to it, like punctuation at the end of a sentence provides closure this presence provides a foil to my existence. Gilberto has his door closed. I peer over Lolita's shoulder as it opens to her call, to a small man, face creased with darkness and a wide smile. We are in, and I look around, to see what the morning sun can illuminate. The floor is cement, pocked here and there and uneven in its support. No bathroom, but a sink, an enormous bathtub-like sink that can be found in old stables, but this one is stained orange from chili powder. I look up to a rustling in the eaves. Soft silhouettes of green come into focus as my eyes adjust. Parrots! I exclaim. Gilberto says something to Lolita. He says, she translates, that they fly in from the heat. He feeds them, they stay for a time, then they fly away again. Some keep returning. Where will they go now, I think, when the place is leveled? I see them following Gilberto . . . harmless vultures, flying in green circles above his path. . . . A wooden chair leans against the sink, before it a plywood table upon which a basin, gray towel, scissors, razor, and soap await the first customer. Gilberto leaves to finish stoking the fire out back, and I can look around less self-consciously. He will bring back hot water for tea, but for now I am absorbed with the smells of the place, a large box of spices it seems, and with the light feathers tumbling silently across the floor, blown by warm draughts of dusty Texas air, with smells of animals I cannot put a name to only know that it is animal that makes my nostrils expand. There are racks for food and spices, a cooler for refrigeration, some heavy blankets in a corner, and candle wax in stalagmite sculptures on every window ledge. Turning, I look behind me, and start to see three helium balloons—red, yellow, green—floating close to eye level. I ask Lolita to make sense of this for me. He found them outside, she says, twisted up on the telephone wire. He climbed up and rescued them. They appear to be approaching me in welcome, bobbing to the left a few times, then to the right. They are alive? I wonder, as they come within a foot of me, then stop, as if not to invade the space that has grown larger around me since my body grew. I put out a tentative hand, grasp the main string that holds them together, hold it for a moment, feeling the pull against gravity. I let go, and the balloons float over our heads. Gilberto comes back with a pail of boiling water and I feel calm, ready to accept his generous offer of tea and *capirotada*.

SAY BRIDGITTE, PLEASE

———

The day was unusually humid, the air muffling the sounds of birds and animals—sounds that, on clear days, would be carried over the miles of flat land. Bridgitte walked along the road near her house, stopping to kick at the chunks of tar that had broken away and were lying to the side. She whistled through the gap in her front teeth, pulling the heads off the black-eyed Susans lining the road as her fingers passed through them. Soon, a ragged path of petals, already browning in the sun, trailed behind her.

Telephone poles, strung together with wire, leaned over cow pastures and fields. Planted among the crops, they grew branchless and towered against the horizon.

In four more days, Bridgitte would see Gem at church. "Goddamn. Four more days." Cursing got rid of some of the frustration she always felt during the solitude of summer. She could see her friend only on Sundays or at church barbecues; they lived too far from each other.

She began to sing, "Boring, boring," to "My Darling Clementine," one of the songs she had taught herself to play on the school guitar. She pictured the guitar now, and her fingers on the frets and strings. She kept her nails clipped during the school year, just so she could play the guitar more easily. It was stored in the back of the auditorium, where she'd found it one day while cutting English.

She didn't like to cut English. She loved to hear the teacher read aloud, no matter what was read. She just enjoyed the sounds of the words working together. But one day she had passed a note, folded like a frog, to Gem. Mrs. Stanton had seen, confiscated it, and read the message to the class. "Dear Gem, MUST tell you about the snake boy I met at the fair Saturday. What a gorgeous hunk! I got him behind the snake tent. Gotta tell you later! Love-n-Stuff, Bridge."

So she'd cut class the next day; she couldn't face everyone so soon. It hadn't been hard to find a place to hide. She knew how to go through a door in the custodian's closet to get to the back of the dark auditorium stage. And it was while she sat in the dark closet, choir robes brushing her hair, that her foot had accidentally come up against the guitar. The jangle of the strings had startled her. But since then, whenever Bridgitte cut class, she would hide in the closet and pick out a song on the strings. She wanted to play something fancy or popular, but all she could manage was "Clementine." She'd never been caught, even the few times she'd sneaked out to play on the empty stage, but she played softly just in case.

"Boring, boring." Bridgitte stopped walking, pulled out her tube-top to blow air between her sweating breasts. She felt a drop slide down her stomach. The tube-top snapped back.

She lifted the hand that wore a birthstone ring and held the ring up to one eye. Peering through a facet, she watched the landscape take on an amber tint. She imagined what it would be like if everything always looked this way—golden colored. She often wondered what it would be like if things were different. When she was sick, she would lie in bed and stare at the ceiling and pretend that she lived right side up in an upside-down world. All of her furniture sat on the ceiling and when she walked into the room, she had to step over the doorway. The windows were lower, and she liked the feeling the strangeness of the whole picture gave her.

And sometimes, when she awoke during the night and it was pitch black outside, and all she could hear were crickets and tree frogs, she would wonder how things would be if John hadn't died. Her dad would tell jokes and drink his beer at home. And if he hadn't died, her mom would talk to her, answer her questions. And when she didn't want to think of it all anymore, she would lie awake listening to the tree frogs chirping and calling. The male would call, then the female. And the chirps would get closer and closer together, till they found each other.

Bridgitte dropped her hand and kicked a chunk of tar. The sting felt good as her big toe hit the hard rock. She heard a noise behind her ear and turned her head. Down the road, emerging from shimmering heat waves, came a large white truck. It moved lazily; like a large white elephant, Bridgitte thought, settling down beside the road. The driver cut the engine. She saw a figure get out and heard the door slam.

She walked back toward it. She could just make out that the figure was a man.

She adjusted her top and pulled her creeping underpants down and wished it wasn't such a hot day. The sweat poured out of her, collecting at the end of her eyebrows and under her lip.

She felt the heat from the metal body of the truck when she got close to it. The man had reached the top of the telephone pole by the time she got there. He supported himself with a heavy belt wrapped around the wooden trunk.

Bridgitte moved to keep the sun out of her eyes and to try to see what he looked like.

"Hi."

He looked down. "Hi."

The voice was young and, from what she could see under the shade of the hard hat, so were the face and body.

"What're you doing?"

He didn't answer her right away. She almost asked again when he said, "Repairin' the wire. Some bird's pecked through the covering."

Bridgitte heard a roughness in his voice that reminded her of the snake boy. "Birds do that?"

"Birds 'n' squirrels."

"Oh."

She watched him, squinting her eyes against the glare. Once, the sun caught the shiny surface of the hat and she had to look away. "You almost done?"

Again he paused, then, "Yeah."

He climbed down, looking alternately at each side of the pole, placing his feet on the pegs.

From what Bridgitte could see of him he looked pretty good: freckled tan, small rear tucked snugly into his khaki pants.

He put the belt and equipment on the passenger seat of the truck, and leaned through the window frame.

"Boy." He took off the hat and ran the back of his arm over his forehead, then shook the sweat to the ground. "It's hell workin' in this shit weather."

Bridgitte blew upward at the bangs hanging over her eyes. They flew up and settled back. His hair was plastered to his head, but she liked the way he looked. She tried to think of something to say to keep him from leaving.

"Don't you get a break?"

"Yeah."

"When?"

"Whenever." He leaned further out the window. "I wanna eat my lunch now, but there're no trees around."

"What d'ya need a tree for?"

He looked at her. Bridgitte imagined that her stomach jumped with excitement at that moment. "For shade."

She looked around. "There's shade on this side of the truck."

"Yeah. Guess it's as good a place as any."

He settled down with his back against the truck. Bridgitte sat in the sun, her legs stretched out, shaking her hair out of her face every so often; she knew it had red highlights that shone when she shook it.

After he finished his sandwich, he asked, "So, what're you doing here?"

"Just walking."

He looked down the road, squinted, and ran his tongue over his teeth to clean them. She watched the tongue roll around as a lump in his cheek.

"So, where're you from?" she asked in return, shaking her hair.

"Planesville."

"That's the next city over, isn't it?"

"Yeah, where the company is. You've never been there?"

"No." She threw a pebble in the air, let it fall to the ground. "I heard it's nice."

"Guess so."

"Is it big?"

"Sort of, bigger than this ol' town."

"I heard they have a new restaurant."

"Yeah."

"Our town doesn't have a real one. There's just the bar, the pizza place, and Mister Donut. Well, now it's Mis Donut, 'cause the lights in the 'ter' haven't been working for a year." She looked up and he was watching—almost squinting—at her. "Do you play the guitar?"

"Huh?"

"I do." She looked at her pink toenails, wiggled them, and told him how she had found the guitar. "Are you married?"

He shook his head and made a face. "Nah. Almost was. She was coyote ugly, ya know? I got out of it just in time."

Bridgitte flinched. Her father and his friends and the boys at school said that—"coyote ugly"—when they talked about a woman they thought was too ugly to be around. Every time she heard them say that she pictured a coyote leg torn to shreds, the animal trying to cut off the leg and the pain from the jaws of the steel trap.

"Well, gotta go." He gathered the remains of his lunch.

Before he could stand, she was up; hand on his arm, she bent over, breasts hanging and pushing against her tube top. His eyes went to her chest. She leaned further over.

"Can we go for a ride?"

"A ride?" He looked up. "Sure."

They got in the truck and drove in the direction in which Bridgitte had been walking. Everything looked different from the elevated seat. She looked down on the flowers and tangled fields, and felt larger than they.

The scenery changed little. An occasional, dusty-leaved tree or low-crawling weed grew between the fences and asphalt. Bridgitte chattered about Gem, and the joke they had made up about Planesville girls losing their virginity in cucumber patches; and she talked about English, guitars and snakes, but didn't mention the traveling snake boy. "My name's Bridgitte. What's yours?"

"Jim."

He drummed on the steering wheel with his fingertips.

"I know a good place to park," she said.

"Where?"

"It's up a little ways, off the side road." The breeze from the open window cooled her off, but she was beginning to sweat again.

She showed him the dirt road, rutted with tracks from other trucks and farm equipment.

"The granary's abandoned now. Mr. Jehnsen sold it about seven years ago. The people who bought it don't use it."

The truck shifted noisily from side to side, trying to ride over the weals of dried mud, baked hard from the heat. Bottles and Mister Donut bags and cups littered the edges of the drive.

He pulled the truck up next to a tall wooden silo, connected to a low building. Painted names and messages graced the lower parts of the structures, and a few dark holes pierced the stained panels. Bridgitte scanned the faded words: "I love you Margie, Love, Timmy." Under it was the reply: "Got to hell Timmy, Love, Margie."

Jim shut off the engine and she turned to him, expecting him to start on her. He opened the door and stepped down.

"Where're you going?"

"C'mon." When she didn't follow, he stopped and smiled. "I want to look around first."

She reluctantly left the truck. The land was used as a dumping ground for the local's trash. Rubber tires with black-eyed Susans and thistle growing out of the centers reminded Bridgitte of the large tractor tire her mom used as a planter. She diverted her thoughts from her mother by examining a couch with its springs bursting from the seat. Broken glass—green, blue, amber—covered everything and made her think of sprinkles on an ice cream sundae. She stopped to pick up a piece of crockery that caught her eye. A slug clung to the bottom. She knocked it off. The fragment had once been part of a plate, with a pattern of daisies and wild roses twining around the edge.

Ahead of her, Jim kicked an empty oil drum. The sound reverberated and bounced off the side of the granary. She began to feel that things were taking too long, so she caught up with him amidst a pile of refrigerators, belly-up, covered with honeysuckle vines.

She pulled a white flower from the vine. "Have you ever done this?"

"What?"

He watched her as she pinched the end of the tube, exposing the pistil. She pulled it out gently, bringing with it a drop of fragrant juice. Lifting it to her lips, they looked at each other as she licked the drop off.

"Here, try one."

She snipped off a golden flower. "The yellow ones are even sweeter." She held it up to his mouth.

He licked the flower, then began to lick her hand. She held it there, feeling his tongue slide between her fingers. He leaned down to kiss her and pressed her shoulder.

She resisted. "Here?"

"Here."

She thought of the clean truck, but he kept pressing, so she sank down.

Lying with her back rubbing against dirt, and her eyes staring up at the cloudless sky, she tried to hold him, but he would never be still long enough; he kept moving over her.

She said his name over and over, but he never said hers. "Say Bridgitte, please, say Bridgitte," she pleaded inside.

He said everything but her name. She tried to remove herself to a place where the light was all golden and Jim was holding her and whispering. But her ears couldn't keep out the obscenities, and she closed up. He didn't notice and finished without her.

He rested; she stared until her eyes felt dry. He stood, zipped his pants, and looked down at her. "Ready to go?"

She didn't respond, but looked past him.

"You want a ride back or not?

She clenched her hands.

"You sure you don't? . . . Well, I gotta get back to work. It was fun." He walked back to the truck, and Bridgitte made one last attempt.

"Jim," she called, "good-bye."

"Bye."

She turned her face away, resting her cheek on the earth and trampled weeds. She heard the engine rev up, settle, then gradually fade as the truck drove off. The cloud of dust it kicked up eventually wafted across her vision. She listened till she couldn't hear the engine anymore, and still she listened.

The sun was lower. She had stopped sweating, but could still smell him on her skin. She plucked a few flowers from the vine near her head and lay them on her chest to cover the scent.

The shadow of the granary slowly crept over her feet, then her legs. And when her body was almost completely in the shade of the silo, as it covered her eyes, she blinked and sat up.

She looked at the packed earth, damp with her sweat, and she took a finger and spelled B-R-I-D-G-I-T-T-E in the soil where her back had been.

CATALPA

⟼

My father. This is who he is: He is a man who grumbles all autumn at the catalpa tree that shades our side porch. The long, dry, weapon-like pods fall as if they were calculating an insult to his sensibilities, conspiring to keep him raking all spring. Cursing them for knowing how to escape the tines of his rake, he says, *Not like leaves*, which know how to give themselves up into his swift, harried movements. *No*, he says, *these damn pods slip right through, like they know*. He carts bushel after bushel to the back of the property. The next day a wind drops more, pushing some end-first into a lawn that is soft from recent snowmelt. The pod shells stand erect, and he goes about bending and pulling at them as if he were pulling at Excalibur, while my mother watches and shakes her head and smiles, knowing he will come in after an hour or so to complain over lunch. He is a man who sighs deeply when the sweet-smelling flowers start to quit their hold, drift down like a heavy snow, wither, and stick to the banisters and porch floorboards, leaving sepia shadows behind when he attempts to brush them off the white paint. And then the sugary droplets appear, sticky residue from the aphids that feed off the catalpa flowers, and he is there again, scrubbing and cursing at the mildew that erupts and spreads, like black crystals expanding, in the sap that is tacky hard.

My father. This is who he is not: He is not a man to pass by the porch's windows and ignore the catalpa after a summer downpour, when the large, elephantine leaves catch and hold the morning's hard rain, and the sky clears, and the sun comes out bringing with it a breeze, which knocks the rain off the leaves and sends the water spilling, so that it looks like it is raining liquid sunshine only under the catalpa, not anywhere else on Earth.

WHERE THE DOG STAR NEVER GLOWS

—

That night, dawn light seeping into dark, Cap did not walk home from the No. 9 mine. He lurched, he hobbled, like a wind-up toy running down. It was the furious cold wind blowing in from the north that took his denim overalls till they crackled like heavy, encased tree limbs after an ice storm. It blew them stiff to freezing hard, the ear-pleasing beauty of the tinkling noise he made walking lost in the pain of it. Pain, Cap knew, took many forms, and this creeping cold was just one more test of endurance. To make it home, the hope that hung out there at some future point, was a good cover-up to the here and now.

"One more mile, y'old bastard," he whispered over crystal formations of exhalation encrusting the scarf he tucked his chin behind. As far as he could concentrate, his carbide lamp cut the dark. And that was not very far.

He had managed this frozen walk home before. But this time, surroundings seemed to pass by more slowly. He realized he was nearing the end of those days when the body is invincible. Not much longer could he kneel with his friends, cutting coal in water, pushed into the "hoot owl" shift and ten hours of overtime by a company too cheap to run its pumps.

This night is warm, summer, the dark being used as cover. Young Cap is trying not to disturb the gravel by the tracks. Moonlight reflecting on a shiny surface the only way to distinguish coal from rock. Up in the hills, his older brother Joshua is coal cracking, working on an exposed vein. Joshua will be caught by the coal and iron police. For two bags of chipped coal, meant for Mother's cookstove, Father will be fined 20 percent off the top of his paycheck for a year, for the chips stolen from the company.

Young Cap will continue to haunt the tracks, trying hard to be a ghost, to be vapor, to succeed where his brother failed.

He knew he was not walking on solid foundation. The ground was hollow, gutted, catacombs of giant ant tunnels twisting beneath a surface held up by columns of coal left for the purpose of being pillars to the earth's crust. His feet were going on him. No need to fear falling through, he was walking on air, suspended. His mind was beginning to feel airy, drafty, too. Randomly, Jesus came to mind. Thoughts of the young Lord walking on water, how it must have felt like this . . . Jesus and the fish . . . fishing. He missed fishing, the quiet, the joy in doing nothing. Father: "Keep quiet and maybe the fish'll go away." An excuse to be aboveground, feeling heat, sun, light, and shadow playing on the eyelids. Father singing: "'Tis little of the world I know, and care less for its ways, for where the dog star never glows, I wear away my days." Healthy seems an unreachable distance away when you're sick—a memory of warmth and light seemed impossible right now.

Coal dust takes away the breath. Cold in winter and dust in summer sends Father into coughing fits. The boys grow used to the sound, static on a radio someone has forgotten to shut off and ignores, in the background, only bothersome if one lets it be. But one hot July, when hot wind turns dust devils on the road and pushes the dry dirt in through the front windows onto Father's resting chair, the coughs send Cap running for Mother. They return to find

Father on the floor, still coughing, pants dark with urine and flooring stained with bursts of red.

From some points above the crows began to waken. He became aware of them, their shapes slowly gathering. As the sky behind them lightened, they materialized from the gray background, black sentinels. As Cap crackled and chimed his slow advance, they loomed and cawed. Like spiders on a dying bush, they know, he thought. How do insects know something is weak, know to attack? He wanted to shoot the birds, every damn one of them. He didn't need them laughing.

The company discovers a large vein of anthracite the morning of June 12, 1929, in the No. 8 mine. Cap and his brother are awakened at 3 a.m. and ordered to work early. In its eagerness to mine the coal as quickly as possible, the company sends thirty-four sleep-deprived, dazed men into the shaft. At 5:35 a.m., some tired worker cross-cutting through the vein forgets to shout the warning. Cap is chiseling at a large, fist-size rock of coal when he is suddenly lifted, carried on the shock waves of explosion, thrown down hard on his back under a heavy rain of black gold. Cap is lucky. His only mark of the accident is a myriad of blue tattoos, spatterings of coal powder that were rocketed into his left cheek. But his brother, closer to the south tunnel, is pinned to a timber, fatally, arms outstretched like Christ. Mother sees the black ambulance with the red cross speed by her sitting room window, watches it disappear in road dust kicked up by its urgency, and she knows.

It was a strange feeling to walk the road alone that night, with morning creeping up from the horizon. He began to feel as if he didn't know where he was; he was not connected to anyone or anything. That the bridge he now scuffed over, patches of ice formed in the wood grooves, was not the same bridge he had crossed the day before. And the day before that. He wished for companionship, though his lips were too numb to move and form words. But he had long left his co-workers behind, the younger miners turning off earlier in the road to the houses set down closer

to the mines. He was still in the old part, living in the shantytown
built in 1859 when oil was discovered in Titusville.

*Blackness everywhere—the color of the ambulance that ferries the dead and
injured, the color of mens' faces, the color of womens' eyelids who stand their
ground and go to work at the plants, despite the black hands that bruise them,
the color of lung disease, the color of the dust that settles on white hanging
sheets, the color of the clouds that seal the sky, the color of the earth and trees,
still stained by tar and grease from when the oil wells flowed richly.*

*Black, too, the color of Alma's hair, pulled back and polished for the
dance. Cap pays his 25 cents at the door, eager to be in the center of the band's
range, a sound swell of scratching, plucking, exhaling bluegrass. Alma coyly
waits by the punch bowl, nervously stroking the elbow of one arm bent across
her flat stomach. That part of her will expand many times under Cap's gentle
attention, and bring forth Jonas, Stephen, Natalia, and Christian. And the
parents will watch their three boys board a train and wave good-bye, the first
generation of Weidmans to leave Titusville, to return to the place from whence
they came, to fight against their own in a war of grand and fatal proportions.
Natalia will be amongst the women who wait, preparing bandoliers and bullet
belts, wondering at the chests and waists that would fill them. They are resigned
to losing men—it's just how things are—and expect to grow old alone.*

The long row of mining houses slowly took form in the distance,
just as the line of crows had earlier, their unnatural silhouettes
pushing back against what was once dew now rising up as pre-
dawn mist. Cap could feel the anxiety that swam around his heart
subside. He had beaten the ice and cold, survived the frost that had
settled within. The crows' cries grew faint—they had no wish to
stray out of the wooded territory, leaving him to his world while
falling back to theirs.

Something else was forming out of the dark. It appeared grayish
white, but the shape told Cap it was a manmade star in the sitting
room window. He stopped. The ice in his clothes took another
moment to catch up to him, to settle their sounds. Five points of a
star. A star that would be golden in better light. Not a star of

Bethlehem guiding everyone to life, but a death star, hung to announce the untimely passing of one of his sons. A new symbol of death fast replacing the ambulance's cross, cutting into the new generation. Alma must have gotten notification last night. The company had left him to tunnel in the dark while his wife took the news alone.

Cap found himself before his front door. He studied the rusty hinges, the screen that was torn in the upper left-hand corner, the way the paint peeled like fish scales, a mossy green up close. The handle lost after years of being pulled open by hands made rough by weariness and unhappy resignation, the spot where it had been nailed in blackened and oily from palms pulling the frame open. Sometimes, he wonders how it all holds together.

He approached this entrance to his home, leaned against the loose mesh but didn't feel it. A whimper escaped and was cut short. In a minute he would go in. In a minute.

ASYLUM

⌐

for A.B.

*M*ae holds both of her daughter's tense hands in her own gloved ones, kisses her taut cheeks, and lets her husband say the good-byes.

"Wonderful time, hon, you take care now. Take care of yourself."

Mae doesn't want to let go, but her daughter pulls away to open the door for them. The sun outside is bright, a severe contrast to the house's dark interior. Mae squints and walks with heaviness to the shiny black Cadillac. Her husband's hand shakes as he turns the key in the ignition. Mae looks across the patch of lawn to her daughter's face, glowing moonlike from the living room shadows. She has someone else to take care of her now, she assures herself. But as the car pulls back and away, Mae has a final, heartbroken thought—that her last touch, the last time she will have touched her daughter, was through the thickness of Sunday mass gloves.

⌐

You'd think with a name like Bliss that I had a good life, wouldn't you? But I was named by my mother more from hope than intuition. She wanted me to have what she knew she would never have. She wanted to protect me in the only small, powerless way she could.

I do remember my father, the sour smell of beer, when he came home, filling the cracks of his calloused hands and sticking to his heavy work boots. I remember a darkness around his face, TV light splashing across his slumped body. The house was always dark then, for June, my mother. Light was a stress for her, and could trigger an "episode," as my father called it. It was he who helped me with my homework, patiently explaining.

He left. I remember thinking for years that it was because I hadn't worked hard enough in school for him, hadn't brought home enough As.

My mother I remember as hardly ever being really present. And she was worse after my father left. In the morning, she'd roll out of bed, make an attempt to brush my hair, then go back to bed. I would go to the bathroom, stand on the toilet lid to see in the medicine cabinet's mirror, and redo the ponytail.

There was never any savior to come lift her up, no one human or being to throw back the curtains and prompt her back into her life. It was all on her to bring herself back from her own dark recesses. And she sometimes succeeded—about a year after my father left, she improved. She applied for Medicaid and SSI and began receiving monthly checks, which helped a lot.

"I'm making sure I have burial insurance, so you won't have to worry, Bliss." She managed a part-time job at home stapling pinwheels together. The company set her up with a machine and the materials, and she'd sit and staple the star-shaped toys all afternoon. They paid $5 for every box she filled. For two years we lived with the shiny stars everywhere—in the sofa cushions, on the floor, scattered on end tables.

These were calm years, years when we rested, instinctively gathering our strength. My mother began to talk to me then, really talk. It was like years of sad, private thoughts were pushing their way to the surface and couldn't be contained.

I would come home from school, throw my bag on the couch,

careful not to crumple any wheels, pour milk and grab a handful of Oreos from the apple-shaped cookie jar. I'd sit with my mother at the kitchen table while she took a cigarette break.

"You take after your grandmother Mae. I wish I had a picture of her so you could see. I didn't think I'd need one, you know? Pictures are for people you're not with, or to capture something you need to remember. I was always with her, she was always around. We were Mae and June, the 'Spring Girls,' as her friends called us. We did everything together." Here she pauses, puts out the Kent and lights another. I stop eating. This is the first time I've heard anything about my mother's life before me. "Then it all changed. I had to watch her become scared of me, ashamed of me. She tried to hide it, but, you know, faces eventually show everything . . . hers kind of shrank into itself. I can't remember too much, lots of blackouts, you know, but there was this one day. It was her turn to have her bridgemates for lunch. She told me not to join them like I usually did, and I heard her say I was out with some 'fellow.' I was supposed to stay in my room. I didn't. I didn't want to be alone. I walked into the living room, and I just remember"—she grinds the base of her palm into her forehead—"I just remember this circle of shocked faces. 'She's naked, Mae!' Then your grandmother threw up, all over the cards, all over the silk bridge cloth."

Another Kent is lit, the last one still smoking in the ashtray. "Oh, she tried. She tried to pretend I wasn't coming apart, her debutante Spring Girl, that the family wasn't. She kept telling me I was just depressed, needed more dates. She set me up with George so-and-so and Michael so-and-so. But word got out what was happening to me, and she couldn't pretend any longer, you know, that I was OK. She felt so guilty. It hurt . . . I hurt . . . and the voices were starting, devil voices, coming from inside me, from *inside* me, Bliss. I tried to end them once. And that's when Mother gave up, she gave me up to the doctors, and the drugs. It was almost a relief, you know . . . but I never thought she'd disappear, that she and Daddy could just drive off one day and leave me." The cigarette trembles, my mother's lower lip dances uncontrollably.

It's hard to feel a parent's pain. You feel protective, sad. And angry. Angry that they can be so vulnerable. You want them to be impenetrable, godlike, and when you find out at a young age that they have feet of clay, it can make you angry forever.

This grandmother, who I could never have a picture of, except to stand in front of a mirror and envision a much older Bliss, haunted me. At night when June wandered the hallways, whispering, trying to keep her thoughts at bay, I lay in bed and imagined Mae, a well-to-do Irish woman with a keen sense of order and polite society, watch the daughter she loved disintegrate into such a burden and embarrassment that she had to flee. I felt abandoned, too. Even though June wasn't yet pregnant when her parents disappeared, still, I was also left, and left with a responsibility that adults couldn't handle. My feelings about Grandmother Mae are, as they are with anything else, mixed and messed up. I am furious with her for hurting my mother, for hurting me. Yet as I listen to my mother mutter as she passes my bedroom door for the eighteenth time, "People are meant to be broken," I am also envious.

But I was never scared until that day in the kitchen when I learned that June was not always as she was now. Schizophrenic, I mean. It came on when she was seventeen, just four years older than I was at the time. Like a slow cancer, it took over her mind. She told me she met my father during one of her "well" periods, after she'd been discharged. She'd married him in a flurry, trying to beat out the next episode. My father saw a pretty, manicly cheerful, upper-class girl and let her set the pace.

My father once told me the story of how they'd met, for a school report I had to write. It was on a cool October day, he said, that time of year when the changing tone of sunlight enhances and brightens everything. It did this to my mother, creating almost a halo around her chestnut hair. This, in a graveyard, on the day of his own mother's funeral. Even in his grief he'd spotted her across the sea of granite and marble headstones. When the service was over he'd stayed, waiting for his pain to settle a bit in the silence. Till a sneeze broke his concentration and he'd looked up to see the woman with blazing hair walking the path away from him. "I didn't think about it, I just got up and followed."

On my pad of ruled paper, I wrote that my mother and father met on the beach. We do have a wedding picture, tucked away in her underwear drawer, a glowing bride with eyes almost too open, a stocky groom with a protective arm around her tiny waist.

And I think about it sometimes, the real story of how they met, and how he must have thought God was watching over him, answering a lonely prayer he hadn't even formed yet. My mother told him she was visiting a friend's grave. How could she tell him the truth?—that she was drawn to those small, eternal plots, that she would lie on the earth, on the decay, trying to get her balance. He wouldn't know until after they'd married how much the presence of death would hover in their lives, how meeting in mourning would set the scene for the rest of their marriage, that the halo had been another one of nature's nasty tricks.

My own voices are beginning: Could this be you? Will this be you? Did Grandmother Mae pass this curse along to June? Did June pass it to Bliss? Every day, I listen for devils, gage my withdrawal from the outside world. And I begin to live in a tunnel, my future narrowing to a small, distant point I am afraid to see.

I don't have good school memories. I was the young girl who had cooties, the one whose mother didn't bathe her regularly or wash her clothes often enough. There were days I had to go searching through my underwear pile, looking and sniffing for the pair that was cleanest. I was taunted, words hurled at me, until a teacher (I'll never forget her, Mrs. Dufton) gave the abusers a lecture, explaining my situation. While I still remained on the fringes, kids were tolerant, some even nice. So I was able to go along on my own, struggling in class to keep concentration, always working to keep up with everyone after long absences. I couldn't let my grades slip, or it might be a sign my mind was slipping. I threw myself into as many activities as I could find time for. I took care of June with almost a vengeance, you could say. And during high school I read once that schizophrenics hardly date and rarely have sex. So I took care of that, as well.

Today I come home from work and turn on the light switch by the front door and get nothing. No light. I try the lamp by the couch, hear the click, but nothing again. I know the socket will be empty when I feel for the bulb.

The first sign in a downward spiral. I feel my way to the kitchen, find the utility drawer, and press on the flashlight. In the small pool of light I can see the table set for four. One of my mother's delusions, these ghostly guests she is sure will appear for dinner.

I follow the column of light to her bedroom, where it illuminates her prone back. "June," I whisper. She turns, which is good, and squints even in such weak light. I point it at the far wall and stroke her forehead. "Come up. Let's have supper. I'll make you an omelet." She holds my hand and I know to squeeze out every last bit of her presence that I can before she disappears again.

My mother, at her worst, believes she is dead. Somehow her mind, which should be a final haven, betrays her. She is tormented by voices, evil strangers, telling her she is departed and devoid of life. She sees an endless strand of winding sheets fluttering outside on the clothesline. She lies in bed, her arms crossed on her chest. She doesn't eat, her bowel movements stop, her pulse goes down. I monitor it and call the doctor. I've lost many jobs because of the time off, large chunks of my life gone by, measured by heartbeats and second hands.

Countless times I stand on the threshold of her doorway. I can't move forward or retreat. I stand, staring at death. I understand families who pull the plug on their brain-dead relatives. Yet my mother will rise up again, when her voices grow weaker and her spirit stronger, and every time I see this perpetual, tortured resurrection, I move on, with less desire.

I once did a research paper on schizophrenia. Like punishment, I made myself pour over books and charts and pictures. I cried looking at the nineteenth-century etchings of patients in madhouses, hanging by their necks and armpits, being driven like cattle before a lunatic's chariot, enclosed in jail-like crib devices.

I stared at the girl on her back, no room to sit up, one arm reaching out from between the wooden bars. Her tangled hair, her beseeching hand, her frightened eyes.

I read in one of those books that a child of a schizophrenic parent may show symptoms before she is twenty-seven. After that age, she is relatively safe. So how do you live until then?

I do my best to be a good girlfriend. I work hard to get that physical affirmation of touch, dialogue, presence. But I can handle just so much. Physical is easy and sufficient for me, really.

Zachary, Zack for short, is my latest. I met him when I was twenty-two. The best friend of another guy I was seeing. When June first saw Zack's old van pull up in our vacant drive, her comment was, "He'd better not have a mattress in the back." She refused to meet him. In four years, she's never spoken to him. He's only seen her at her permanent place, the kitchen table. At most he gets a cursory nod and penetrating stare. She is feral in her judgment of others. Despite her isolation, she knows people. A survivalist's instincts, I suppose. She knows Zack is her substitute. She knows that when she is dead, he'll take her place.

After I take care of June, I take care of Zack. He's lasted a long time. The last two years I've been seeing only him. I do his laundry and clean his small apartment. On our first date, he refused to tell where he was taking me. "It's a surprise," was all he said. He shifted gears, coaxed and prodded the old van through the gradual darkness, turning off main roads onto small side roads overhung with low branches, which sometimes slapped his windshield. I wasn't scared about anything that might happen to my body back then.

"You have a stuffed fox on your dashboard," was all I said.

"Helps me find my way back to the right van." He smiled.

We came to a halt by a long stretch of chain-link fence. "It's a golf course. Ever been on one at night?"

"I've never been on one at all."

"Come on. You can *feel* the ocean here."

We hopped the fence and made our way over the lawn of rolling man-made hills and valleys, skirted the occasional tree. All color had evaporated to leave gray grass, black trees, white sand, light gray flags waving in the ocean breezes. I could smell the ocean, the salt and the seaweed, just beyond the cliff we were approaching. The water was obscured by the lacy silhouettes of pines, but you knew it was out there, could hear it rolling forward, and, yes, you could feel its great expansion.

It was easy to kiss Zack there, to sink down onto the grass carpet and begin to love him. But just at that moment the rain began, or what I thought was rain. Looking up I saw the underground sprinklers working, sending whirls of cold spray down on us. I ran through the fountains, laughing and slipping, feeling strangely free. When I got home, with stripes of mud on my jeans, June was wandering the hallways. "I had to have a girl," she growled when she caught sight of me. "I'm so sorry for what you're going to go through. So sorry." And she lifted her hands to her head and cried softly, the only time I've ever seen her with such strong emotion.

Zack is trying to kick his cocaine habit. I know what you're thinking, but most of the time he's good. He's in the moment and planning for the future. I've told him I won't marry until I'm twenty-seven. He doesn't ask why, just accepts. That's the trade-off. He just accepts me for what I am—giving, aloof, part of June.

But sometimes everything weighs too heavily, and I decided, last summer, to give up the more expendable burden. He called every day, begged me to come talk to him. Finally, I was drawn back. I took the bus to his apartment. Watching for me, he opened the screen door as I approached. The curtains inside were drawn and the shades pulled down and the familiar odor of stale cigarette smoke and beer seeped out.

I moved into the sunlight, to the porch steps, neutral territory. He came out of the house, arms and shoulders exposed, achingly familiar. I couldn't touch—I'd given up that right.

"So, how have you been?" I asked.

"Terrible—can't sleep. Are you happy to hear that?"

I was afraid of the expression in his eyes, rimmed by green-blue circles.

"How've *you* been? I hope you're having a great time, 'cause I don't know if I'll ever forgive you for this."

I picked at the overgrown grass by the bottom stair, surprised at the new feeling in my stomach that came from feeling wanted. "It's been restful." I finally looked to his face but he was staring at the ground, arms resting on his knees, hands hanging limply.

"Look, it's a rhinoceros beetle. I haven't seen one in years." He took a long finger, dark with axle grease, and touched the back of a bug the size of a golf ball, its black shell shimmering colors of blue and green under the hot sun.

"We used to look for these in the woods. See their sharp jaws? If you can avoid them and stroke them on the back . . . they sit real still."

I watched as he stroked the insect's hard shell. The pincerlike jaws slowly expanded and contracted, but didn't strike.

Zack can't leave me because he depends on me so much. Do you know how important that is?

It's why I put up with the bad days, when he's down to $10 in the bank and needs his vomit cleaned up off the bathroom tiles and walls. I think this is actually when I love him the most, when he's lying in my arms, his brow sweating, his voice a constant moan. Then I feel truly strong.

Since my father left, our small, shingled house has receded into the background of our neighbors' lives. A high grass wall runs deep and thick from the sidewalk along the suburban street to the front cement walk, green and dark with age. Maples and oaks have sprung up from what was once a tidy front lawn; limbs spread out like great arms protecting us from prying eyes.

I'm sure we're a haunted house to some kids, and my mother is a witch. But our direct neighbors, people who remember my father, have been good. They occasionally drop off a tuna casserole or stop by to fix a leak or clean a backed-up gutter. I even opened the front door one day to find three cans of Ragu spaghetti sauce on our stoop, still fresh after a cold November night. Mostly, we accept help. But I left those cans just under our mailbox by the road, so whoever had dropped them off would see, and know.

To me, nature is something to fight. But I gave up the battle on the front lawn, let it, her, whatever, take back its land. Sometimes it seems united in one big conspiracy against my family, and I'm angry at it. I withdraw, like my mother, have to fight with myself to get out of bed in the morning and face another day, another cold sunrise. The problem is, you can't shake your fist at the grand design, you can't scream at your fate.

I do find myself going out to the back garden, which I haphazardly maintain, and the smell of wild Japanese honeysuckle hints to me maybe . . . nature is trying to make up. I sit by the fence, breathing in as much as I can before I lose the scent.

When Thorazine came along, June improved. Her episodes are now further apart. But just as the extremes flattened out, the lows remain more constant. She never leaves her nightclothes or the house, even for cigarettes. In spring she is hot and in fall she is cold. I see her body as loose and sagging because of the lack of containment over these latest years. No tight elastic or underwires or fabric boundaries to keep her in proper alignment. When June awakes from sleep, simply steps out of her bed into the daytime, she is still clouded over with hazy delusions. Her spot is by the kitchen window, at the Formica table, a pack of Kents just by her shaky hand. Smoke plumes around her fragile, flowered nightgown, and the square, bar-shadowed patch of sunlight from the window passes over, by, and away until it disappears, when late afternoon takes over and she's finished the pack.

On my twenty-sixth birthday I awake to a day so sharp it hurts my eyes to look out the window. The sky, electric blue, drops a white fire over the landscape. I squint and rush outside, still in my nightshirt. My narrowed perspective takes in the small yard, the tangled, untended rose and honeysuckle bushes, the elm, and the mermaid statuette beneath.

It is a good day for a birthday. The statue reminds me of a birthday past when I had begged my father, after reading *The Little Mermaid*, for a mermaid of my own. He had wracked his brains for a suitable form. Finally, he'd gone to Frank's nursery and special ordered it. On another bright, August day, he'd wrapped a bandana around my eyes and led me to this spot under the old elm, and, rather embarrassed, presented me with the topless gift.

I walk across the dry grass. Grasshoppers whirr out of reach, cicadas buzz. The heat of the day is already warming my hair. In the sudden shade of the tree, I stroke the mossy head of the forever-smiling girl. I am glad to have something solid left of happier times. When June eventually dies, for real, I know there will be nothing left behind to make me smile like I am smiling at this moment.

"Happy Birthday, sweet thing." Zack rolls his arm over the scene before him—an enormous rock takes up the clearing in the woods. "It's a glacier rock. Moved here about X-X-X years ago."

"A rock?" I ask, puzzled.

"Bliss, you've missed so much. I want you to see something that's bigger than all of us."

"On my birthday? You want me to feel small on my birthday?"

"No, no. Come here." Zack is pulling himself up on the basalt ledge, reaching down a hand. I find footing in a crumbling crevice and push up.

"Just touch it, Bliss." We are standing on a natural ledge, in actuality a piece of the large monolith that broke off of its pendulous belly. I know I'm supposed to be feeling something important through my hand, but instead my eye is caught by the blackened remains of a campfire at our feet, and the small, almost timid graffiti above in yellow chalk: "I Love MT." In my imagination I feel the passion, once absorbed, now emanating from the flat ledge where they must have lain. It all somehow mocks me, in a way I can't share with Zack, even. A long-buried memory rises up.

"You know, someone at school actually threw me a party when I turned twelve. Her mother baked a beautiful vanilla cake, pink-ice rosebuds all over it. When she carried it in, and they all sang to me, I felt so good. Like I belonged. Then they handed me the knife, and I began cutting. The room got real quiet. I looked up to see my friend's face, all changed. Her mother's the one who told me you were supposed to blow out the candles first. Can you imagine that? I didn't even know that much."

"Bliss." Zack puts his arms around me. I feel myself go stiff, already longing for the walk back through the woods to home and safety.

A week before Christmas I unpack the ornament box slowly. There are few ornaments for our fake tree, a silvery concoction that I saw poking out from a trash can years ago on my way home from school. We had not had a tree for two years after my father left. I miss the ritual of freezing toes and fingers, apple-red cheeks, words of argument over which tree is better frozen for a short time on my scarf.

I know the silver tinsel is ugly, but anything bright makes me feel better. I hang the Styrofoam balls, Betsy Clark figures glued and sprinkled by smaller hands. The pipe cleaner hooks are yellowing. A few plain, colored bulbs left over from past Christmases.

I have to be careful only to put on the lights when June isn't around, for the bright-colored bulbs give her a headache. Now I hear her slippered feet whispering down the hallway leading into the living room, so I pull the plug.

She enters, rubbing her forehead, glancing at the tree with a noncommittal look.

"You want to hang something?" I ask.

She doesn't respond, her mind is working on something else.

"Why are you wasting yourself on Zack?"

"What?"

"Zack. I want to know about Zack, and why such a smart girl is with him."

I place the hooked wire of a red ball over a branch, then pick another from the yellowing dividers. The question surprises me. June never even speaks Zack's name.

"What good does being smart do me if I never leave this place? I'm so out of it, so behind. Zack's way ahead of me in some ways, ways that keep me interested." I don't want to see her face. I hang a blue bulb.

The sound of a match strike, the fizz of immediate flame, the smell of smoke, and the exhale, longer than usual.

"You know I was headed for college? Number nine in my class?"

"Yes, I'm sorry."

"You know what it's like to be near death, and have nothing?"

"No."

"Bliss, it's almost as bad as death, the life I've led."

"You must have some good memories."

"Memories? Poof! That's what they do when you get old. You want something more solid. What I'm trying to say here, Bliss, is you're the one good thing I can leave behind. You're my only accomplishment. And Lord knows I had little to do with you, too . . . Bliss . . . look at me. I'm only saying this once. My head's clear for the moment. I want to say this. This is your mother talking to you."

My palms and underarms are sweating. My mother is looking directly at me, into my eyes.

"You're better than all of this. Me. Zack. I'm near the end, I know it. Don't trade me in. Don't swap your crazy mother for a sick man. Get your own life, please." June reaches out a hand. I look at that hand, a claw, and pull back.

"I'll be all right, OK? I can take care of myself fine." I escape from the room to my bed, bury my head in my pillow. Her smoke has absorbed itself into my hair, and I scream quietly. It's too late for a mother.

"Hey, it's a blizzard out here. I gotta plow near your house. Want to come along?"

"Yes," I answer Zack. "See you soon."

The low rumble of his pick-up truck pulling up lets me know he's arrived. I pull on a wool jacket and gloves and wrap a scarf around my head. His truck has no heat.

I often join Zack during his moonlighting hours. In the winter, he works as a subcontractor plowing the roads. I like the height of the seat, the power of the plow as it pushes snow out like whipped cream, the rush and speed of the snow against the dark window.

"You look pretty tonight," he says, a quick glance sideways.

I know my nose is red and my hair sticking out in all directions beneath the staticky scarf.

"I got a raise at work," he says.

"Yeah? Great. How much?"

"About $50 a week. It's enough now, you know? To start thinking about things."

"Things."

"Yeah, things. Like you and me getting married."

"Married?"

"Yeah, Bliss, married. Don't sound so pleased."

"I'm just surprised. I didn't expect anything, I mean, I did expect someday, maybe, when I'm twenty-seven—"

"Aw, Geez!" He slaps the steering wheel. "I should've known it would go this way."

The truck speeds faster.

"Slow down, Zack, it's OK, don't get mad. Slow down. Of course I want to marry you. I'm just surprised, is all."

"After four years?" The truck slows.

"Surprised you want to get married. You're still doing coke—"

"No, I stopped, this time for good. I promise. I got money in the bank now. I'm ready for this. I want kids, lots of kids. We're running out of time, Bliss." He glances sideways. "And you know, you seem OK. . . ."

The snow is rushing at us harder, denser. The sound of the plow scraping asphalt fills my ears. I watch the snow throw itself onto people's front lawns and driveways, snow that will be hard chunks of gray ice by tomorrow that you'll have to dig through to get out. I wonder about you people within the warm, yellow light of the windows we pass. I try hard, but I can't see the future. No vision, just the speeding, dark tunnel enveloped in his headlights.

There's no asylum for me, I think. No place of rest.

Sunday Drives

–

*I*t was what we did every Sunday for many years, while our
neighbors sat in church pews. My father insisted on piling our
family into the car for a drive. Destination is unimportant, he said.
What matters is that we are all together. In his own way, he was
worshiping America's roadside stops and tree-lined vistas from the
dashboard of his '63 Thunderbird—the 'Bird, as we came to call it.

Togetherness was my father's dream. It was something he worked
for on those afternoons. Today I know more about his lonely
childhood, but then his need only felt like a burden, to always be
happy with each other. When my younger sister Gracie and I fought
in the back seat, claiming our territory with a sacred line imagined
down the center of the car's interior, my father grew upset. My
mother, with two sisters of her own, would repeat that it was normal
for siblings to fight. Not in my family they don't, he'd say. I could
feel the anger in the way the car moved, sharp and abrupt, and I
sensed it was time to quiet down.

I think it's accurate to say the '60s was the final decade when
most middle-class families had just one car, mainly for the father's
use. It was the same in our family—my mother, basically, was

stranded during the week. She relied on the soaps and her neighbors for distraction, and had to be content to live a life of waiting—for her children to come home from school, for her husband to come home from work. I still see her rushing to open the door, see her standing and waiting for my father, weary from his job as a plumbing engineer for Grumman, shoulder bent with the heavy contents of his briefcase. She would take his felt hat and overcoat, so eager to show her love in this way. My father insisted on kissing each one of us hello, another ritual to show our togetherness.

I remember my father as being a great lover of hats. He wore one even while mowing and raking. When preparing for Sunday drives, he would pull from the hall closet a canvas hat, decorated with a checkered ribbon around the brim. It spoke of the breezy casualness with which he took these trips. My mother wore her gauzy scarves, triangular folds tied beneath her chin, looked bug-eyed in her large, round Jackie O. sunglasses.

Aside from these items, my father's idea was to leave the house with nothing—no purses, no toys, no food or umbrellas. He did bring his alligator wallet, with special money set aside for whatever might come up. Learn to be yourself, without props and supports, he preached. Learn to be free of it all. Learn you don't need things, but be grateful to go back to them.

My memories of the early drives are sweet and filling. Long Island's moving panorama of forests and harbors, strip malls and farmstands never grew tiring. But sometimes the 'Bird's blue, polished exterior, catching the sun, and the warmth building up within lulled me into a light sleep. The car rocked around bends, lifted over waves of unrepaired frost heaves and ruts, and sailed smoothly along the Long Island Expressway. My parents' voices grew small and distant, muffled as if from the far end of a tunnel, but soothing in the sound they created together.

As the day darkened we returned with our plunder—homemade doughnuts and buckets of hand-picked strawberries; wooden boxes of Big Boy tomatoes; brown bags of butter and sugar corn; mulled cider and warty gourds; Coney Island prizes and cases of NeHi orange soda. Gracie and I still laugh over the dinner my mother once bought in the spirit of trying to match my father's adventurousness—a tin bucket of clams and mussels, layered between seaweed, along with another bucket of live crabs. Once home, the crabs made their escape into the back garden, and Gracie and I were commanded to retrieve them. We went about reluctantly, pulling the AWOL creatures from beds of daylilies and from beneath the chain-link fence that bordered our neighbors' yard. At dinner, they stared up at us from our plates with boiled eyes that still managed to recriminate.

These drives began in spring, fresh with expectancy, and ended in fall, as we prepared for the coming cold. I do remember my father's arm around my mother's shoulders, her playing with the short hair that escaped beneath his hat. But mostly I remember that summer when I watched, from the back seat, my parents' marriage slowly fall apart.

It began with a subtle shift in positions. After a summer of fried clams in paper cartons, Carvel cones, poor rain and heat storms, I noticed my mother now looked out her window, always to her right, never ahead or to her left, where my father now drove, gaze fixed forward, silent, both hands on the wheel.

And as Gracie and I instinctively quieted, children hoping somehow to repair the tense atmosphere, they began to fight. Little, nasty jabs at first. I'm tired of not knowing where we're going, I need to know. Can't you plan a day for once? Why do you have to control the money? Roll down the damn window so we can get some air in here, forget your damn hair. Then as the weather cooled and the sun lowered, bursts of hot-edged, unpredictable anger frightened us into pushing as far away as we could into the corners of the cold, leather upholstery.

When my father grabbed his hat one Sunday, I reluctantly followed, stomach queasy. It was a bright fall day, the leaves completely transformed. The yelling began immediately, the car jerked forcefully in our lane, and I banged on my mother's shoulder, yelling, I have to throw up! The 'Bird veered over to a halt with a screech of rubber, and I pushed down the handle, jumped into the high, sour-smelling weeds, and let everything go.

My mother never went on another drive again. I sat in her place; Gracie hung dangerously between the bucket seats. My father didn't notice. A pall of silence fell over us—we no longer had to pretend we were happy.

It seemed my father was drawn to desolate stretches of shore, beach roses and wind-sculpted pines repeated over and over. Listen, he finally spoke, the only thing you can be sure of, certain of, is that you'll always love your children. Make sure you girls have children. It's what your mother and I are holding on to right now.

The ocean, on my right, flashed through the trees.

And find something else, he continued, something that can't change—words, nature, God, music, anything. . . .

He slowed, put the turning light on, and pulled over to face the Atlantic, plainly visible, framed by dark, dry scrub. He watched the waves toil endlessly ashore. I watched his face, jawline working, brow shivering, the face of a man whose beliefs have fallen apart in his own hands. And I looked to them, his hands, one alternately caressing and gripping the bright blue plastic of the steering wheel, in the same way that he had held on to us, the other pushing at the dangling keys, as if restraining himself from the urge to continually turn them, to start the engine, or his life. And I knew that, for the first time on a Sunday, not knowing where he was going was a hard, painful thing.

BIRD MAN

*S*he dreams within her dream of a bird trapped in a solarium, filled with partygoers. The bird turns into the perfect man, and as she dances in his arms, she explains her plans to free him out the palladium window. But she turns away from the Bird Man, just for a second, and when she turns back, he is gone. . . .

Today I awoke to a rooster crowing and the chiming of convent bells and the jumble of children's voices reveling below my bedroom window. All happy sounds, and they make me want to apologize.

To my family? My friends? Myself? Yesterday I found myself in St. Servaasbasiliek, and lit two candles. Organ music wended its way into my history, drawing forth doubts. It is music—caught, held, and shot back down to the listener in waves by the carefully designed ceilings—meant to reach even the most resistant of souls. The sounds refuse to be cast too far away.

Taking in the statues, frescoes, giltwork, glory, it seems to me to be too much work for such unworthy beings as us humans. My eyes travel to the cracked tiles at my feet—I can't keep myself from looking to the ground—and I examine the brown clay that is forcing its way back out from behind the green, yellow, black glazing. I had a moment of vertigo, and the senseless thought that I was buried there, just there, at my own feet.

Europe can do this for you, make your spirit feel more ancient and connected. It's something to regret about life back in the States, where I have steadily lost all connections, even to my younger brother, Jimmy.

The school bell rings again, bringing the first period to a close. I've been in bed long enough to see the last weak bit of sun disappear. Another gray day. I ready myself in a bathroom the size of a small closet. The sink barely holds my hands, the hot shower water lasts just a few minutes. Testimony, I think, to the fact that we Americans spend much more time in our bathrooms and on our looks than do people in other countries.

Nelly is in the living room when I step out. "*Dag*," I greet her. She nods. We nod a lot, as she speaks no English. Amazing how far a nod can take you. She hums as she sweeps and dusts. Dried pasta from last night's meal rolls across the floor and she chases it down, her large body, framed in flowery fabric, moving agilely within the confines of the small rental apartment.

Again, I have this urge to apologize—for the pasta, for the dust from my shoes, for the hair I'm shedding in record amounts, for my fingerprints on the mirror. For my confused presence.

I understand now why the Dutch painters developed such a dark style. It isn't just that their glazes have darkened with age. I've awakened to that lead-gray light that lasts the day for almost a week now. Most mornings I sleep through an hour of pale sunshine at 8 a.m. when the cock begins to crow and the newly arisen sun has the strength to pierce the dense fog. But then it's beaten back by a cold rain that falls often from roiling gray clouds, leaving a slippery sheen on stones—cobbled from gray granite—that fan out in the streets and alleys.

Those Dutch oils make sense now. I imagine the artists waited long, shivering and determined, to capture that brief spill of yellow over the ocean's horizon or over a countryside farm. I recognize now how the camaraderie, pipe smoke, bright fruit, glowing cheeks, and hearth fires they sought to capture belied the dark just outside their physical parameters.

It's been dark like this my whole life, so this place suits me fine. I have leaned over the River Maas several times this week, staring into the currents, looking for my father's face, maybe reflecting from the sky from whence he fell.

I grew up on shaky soil. Maybe that's why I keep looking down lately, trying to find a solid place to stand.

Vacation is almost over. Time is running out. I have to visit the memorial.

It's a struggle to open the old kitchen windows, but Mrs. Beechum is determined to let in the new spring breezes, which send the bodies of dead flies and spiders scittering across the mildew-spotted ledges like miniature tumbleweed. She removes the desiccated bodies with a pained look on her face, catching them between shaky fingers by just the tips of their wings or their folded legs, tucked in like the legs of her card table waiting for the next game of bridge. A steady, sharp sound of rock striking rock makes her look out.

Beyond the low hedge of forsythia that divides their properties, she sees her neighbor's daughter, Amy, by herself, on a lawn that is beginning to green. A large rock in one hand, she pounds another rock on the ground between her outstretched legs, forehead knitted in concentration. Mrs. Beechum squints to focus more. The girl is smashing something softer. Acorns rejected by the squirrels from the previous fall harvest?

A plane passes overhead, low enough that for a few moments the sounds of Amy's pursuit can't be heard. And then there is Amy's mother coming out the back door, speaking to Amy and pointing to the sky. Amy continues to pound away, ignores the bare foot her mother uses to prod her leg.

Mrs. Beechum sighs. She wonders why she continues on, an old woman surviving yet another bitter northeast winter. She knows about death and how it ends a life, but not a relationship.

So much seems to be waiting for me at the end of the road to Aachen that I find it impossible to speed toward it. I drive slowly, meditatively, letting others pass. But eventually I pull into the parking lot of the Henri-Chapelle cemetery.

Thousands of bleached-white crosses fan out from the colonnade, and one belongs to my father. You should be with me, Mom, I think. And Jimmy. I shouldn't be doing this alone.

The young man is eating his lunch when I enter the Visitors' Room. He puts down the baguette and wipes his clean mouth primly with a napkin before holding out his hand.

"How can I help you?" He speaks in English with a French accent.

"I'm looking for my father. I was told he is buried here. Major Hollis of the 101st Airborne Division."

"Yes, have a seat, please. Let me look in the record book." He picks up a black leatherbound book and passes his hands over the browning paper, top to bottom, top to bottom. He stops and taps at an entry. "Here he is. Section F."

Section F. One step closer. But there is one more question, one that has been lurking in the background for many years. "I was wondering, umm, why wasn't his body sent home? Do you know?"

"Many times the bodies weren't claimed. Parents didn't want the physical evidence of death. Sometimes, there was not much to return."

"But if my mother had requested it?"

"Ah, then it would have been. The specifics I can't help you with. You would have to contact the Air Force. Are you ready to go? I'll take you there myself."

Our footsteps echo on the marble floor as I follow him back outside.

"There is a chapel there"—he points to a door—"if you wish to visit later."

The entrance to the cemetery is guarded by a monolithic angel, the broad valley behind her wingspan full of a whiteness that must blind the eyes in summertime. Rows and rows of crosses, and the occasional Star of David, shine against the green of the well-maintained lawn. Here and there a linden tree shades a cluster of graves, but most look vulnerable, exposed to the wind and rain.

We turn down a grassy lane. I'm getting closer, and I expect to feel that I will know which one it is. Instead I am surprised when he stops in front of a cross bedecked by a holly wreath. The square plot in front holds frost-bitten remains of some plantings I can't identify. No other graves in the vicinity are decorated.

"Ah, this is one of the adopted graves," my guide says. "You look confused. Some of the graves are adopted as school projects or by community groups. Someone visits your father's grave, since you cannot, and maintains it. I will go back and look it up. I can give you the name of the person, if you like."

I nod, and he leaves.

The grass is brittle and cold. I trace JOHN I. HOLLIS, WILMINGTON, OHIO, with my fingers.

"Hello, Dad, I brought you these." I remove the plastic that covers a bouquet of white roses and lean them up against the cross, push the stems into the dormant garden as best as I can.

What can be gleaned from a plot, a little part of the earth that's been apportioned and allotted and dug into and cradles someone you never got to know? I wait for something to make up for the pain, for some explanation of why my family had to suffer his loss, for some reason why I had to suffer a mother who grew deeply depressed and couldn't be more than a shadow. And I no longer want to apologize, I want someone to apologize to *me*.

The skeletal branches of the lindens scrape and creak in the wind blowing west, into the Berwinne streamlet and into the ridges beyond. I hear my heart beat in my ears. An acidic taste fills my mouth. I feel the hard ground beneath my knees. After a time, I rise. The ground won't yield, it won't give up answers or apologies.

"Coleta De Pre is her name." The young man holds out a slip of paper. "She was home when I called. She tells me your father's plane crashed near her village. She will be home tomorrow and will see you, if you like. There is a map to her house. She speaks English, so you will have no problem."

I look down at the black lines he's drawn, neatly guiding me with small arrows to Liège.

"Thank you. Thank you for being so . . . well, welcoming."

"I hope it helped," were his last words.

High noon in summer, no shadows in the graveyard. The simple granite structures pull in the heat from the sun. Jimmy leans against a tombstone, trying to be small, trying not to breathe loudly.

"Ready or not, here I come!" his sister calls out the harmless threat.

He listens with childish excitement, anticipating discovery. But instead, he hears her bare feet push pebbles along the path in front of the stone until she is past him. Delighted, he settles down into the wild grass, feeling the heat relax him. The whir of insects lulls him to sleep.

"Jimmy!" He looks up startled into his sister's face, disoriented. The tomb now casts a shadow over him and he sees she is crying clean lines of tears from her eyes to her dusty chin. She holds him, cradling him.

"Oh, Jimmy, I couldn't find you. I looked and looked. I didn't know what happened."

He lets her rock him, enjoying the closeness, so tightly held he has to breathe deeply to get air. And he triumphs at having found such a fine hiding place. He is too young to recognize the intense fear in her grip.

Another misty morning ride. I can just see the stone houses that sit by the road. The fields and woodlands behind them are shrouded. I know the structures are there because I saw them one clear morning during the train ride from Brussels. The fields would be very neat and well planned, surrounded by copses of annually pruned, stunted trees. The branches aren't encouraged to spread and give privacy to the owners, like they are in the States. In fact, it's easy to see right into a house or apartment window, right into someone's life, perhaps covered only by a piece of hand-tatted lace. My landlord told me that Netherlanders don't believe in hiding themselves from neighbors. Respectability is extremely important, and windows are expected to be left unobstructed to show that nothing untoward is going on inside that needs to be hidden.

I think of all the hiding my family did. All the things my mother hid from Jimmy and me. But mostly she hid the truth. She kept pretending my father was out there somewhere, flying, just waiting for the right time to come home. For years she looked up whenever a plane passed overhead, watching its smoke trail long before it was out of view, as if it could be her husband's plane that had just passed us by. She lived in a vague way, loved in a vague way. But the worst thing she did was make us believe that our father was somewhere out there, still alive, but just wouldn't come home.

Match hiss. Breath extinguishes flame. The long, desperate drag on the Eve cigarette. "Mystery Theater" is on the radio and Anne doesn't hear her children come home till they are suddenly there, lunch pails clanging on the kitchen's enamel-top table.

Drowning the Eve in a glass of orange juice, she puts her feet into cloth slippers, grabs her nightgown. She usually hears them coming and gets to the kitchen first, pours glasses of milk and puts out a plate of cookies. She shuffles in past them to the beehive cookie jar. Empty. Mrs. Beechum's molasses cookies are finished. She taps her fingernails on the counter. Only a few nails are long enough to make sound as they hit.

"Mom?"

She turns after the second time her daughter calls. "Hmmm?"

"At school . . ." Jimmy leaves for the bathroom. Amy watches him out the door. "Today, Jenny and Sam told me that Dad is dead. That he died in the war."

Faucet drips. Heavy drops on steel ping. The wall clock's tick measures the silence.

"Mom!"

She left the radio on, didn't she? Anne makes her way around Amy. Her bare arm brushes against the girl's sweater and she sucks in her diaphragm to avoid further contact as she passes.

I didn't do much better than my mother. I became a night nurse and spent the dark hours working long shifts, concentrating on other people's sufferings. I didn't want the reality of daylight forced on me; I'd had enough of it.

The little map indicates that I'm almost there. I pass two horses grazing in a frosty field, a winters' growth hazing their outlines. And then I'm in front of a stone house with brown, weblike vines spidering the façade. The vines must sprout ivy and roses in the summer.

Then this little woman, barely up to my shoulder, opens the door. Her hair is salt-and-pepper gray, the kind that grows stiff and wiry with age, hers in a pageboy gone snarly. It gives her a slightly messy appearance, but her clothes are pressed and classically European. I put my hand into a warm, double handshake. I hold out my hostess gift with the other hand.

"*Merci*, Amy. May I call you Amy? I love this brand of *chocolate*." She puts the box on an oaken hallway table, its drawer handles carved in griffin form. "Keep on your coat. We should walk."

Coleta is already pulling on a wool coat and hand-knit mittens. I see a limp tail of carrot greens hanging over the pocket brim. She ushers me back outside.

"I visit my neighbors' horses once a day to bring a treat. Come," she urges, taking my arm and almost pulling me down the road. "I knew someone from the family would come someday. What would I tell them? I used to ask myself. And here now is his daughter. . . ."

She gives a squeeze to my arm. The warmth from her proximity infiltrates my own heavy jacket, coated now with fine Belgian mist, and when she stops abruptly to point across several pastoral fields to a treeline in the distance, I have to back up to her side. "That is where your father's plane went down."

I stare into the framed vista, see nothing beyond trees.

"I know what it is to lose a father."

"I was only three." My voice sounds strident.

We continue to the field where I saw the two grazing horses. A car passes, honks a greeting to Coleta. The morning frost is still frozen, causing the grass to crunch like gravel as we leave the pavement and approach the wooden fence. The animals swing their necks regally and saunter over.

The horse closest to me hangs its head over, nudging and searching. "Here." She hands me a carrot.

Horses scare me. It's the enormity of them, their proportion so much larger than us humans. The great power in them. The teeth. I hesitate, and Coleta says, "Here, like this. He will not bite." She holds the carrot while he breaks it in half; then she positions it so it is flat on her palm, making her hand a plate. The horse's lips pull back, showing its large yellow teeth, and the front lip reaches out and gently rolls the carrot into its mouth.

"Many animals died during the occupation. No food for the poor creatures." Coleta runs her mitten between the horse's eyes and snout. The other horse hangs its head between us and I hold out my carrot as she did. The space between the animal's nostrils is pink and freckled. When they realize there is no more food, they leave.

"I grew up in Haine-St-Pierre, west of Liège. I remember, when word of the Nazis approaching came, we hid all we could. Even tires in the soil so the Nazis would not take the autos with them. The winter was cold. Almost no coal, so we only could heat the kitchen." She smiles up at me impishly. "I keep my house very hot now. My gift to myself."

My toes are tingling in my boots where the tips are buried in the rime. We are quiet for a time, watching the horses retreat, the only sound in the coldness their chewing of frozen grasses and nettles and the whoosh of a passing car. I sense the silence should be filled by her need now, not mine.

"It was 19 . . . 43, yes, 1943, when my father was commanded to be a railroad hostage. He was to report to the station two times a week. He had to go. The Nazis used our men as hostages to get their ammunition and soldiers safely across the border. Allies would not blow up a train with civilians on it. At the end of these days of praying and watching the radio clock, my mother would go to La Louviere to meet the returning train. One day, she did not bring him home. Not one of the hostages came back that day. No one told us why. . . ."

The horses now mirrored Coleta and me in their positions, standing side by side but not touching, vapor from our heated exhalations mixing together. When she seemed done with looking, she turned back toward her home.

"I was eighteen. I needed a man to take care of me. I wanted to get away from Haine-St-Pierre. I married a nice young man who brought me here, to Liège. I became pregnant a month before he was killed in the Battle of the Bulge. Your father crashed in Liège that same day."

"I'm so sorry."

"I am sorry too, Amy."

I look again to the treeline off in the west. White sky, India ink–black branches. Nothing there; the connection is here, beside me.

The kitchen explodes with color, more color than I've seen since arriving in the Netherlands. Red-checked curtains, mustard-yellow horsehair plaster walls, a farm table and mismatched chairs coated with thick, seaglass green paint. A blue enamel kettle simmers on the two-burner stove, seconds away from whistling.

"Tea?"

"Yes, thank you."

"Sit, sit, be comfortable."

The kettle whistles, the water is poured over a metal tea ball that is hung over the lip of a teapot, and I keep my hands beneath the table because they are shaking.

She looks at me for a long moment, studying my face. "I hope it made you happy to see the grave dressed up."

"Yes, it was a surprise. A nice one . . ." And then tears are streaming down my cheeks, silent, continuous like rain, and I cover my face with both hands to hide my embarrassment. I have never let anyone see me cry before.

The cuckoo clock behind me ticks. Coleta uses small silver tongs to drop two sugar cubes into her tea. The sound of the demitasse spoon striking porcelain joins the ticking. The tears run dry, and I can speak.

"I haven't seen sugar cubes in years."

She smiles, pushes what looks like a scrapbook with a tartan cloth cover across the table. I open it at the place where a paper bookmark is inserted.

"That is the only record of your father's fall."

The article is in French and she translates: "'Pilot's Body Identified': The body of an American pilot was identified yesterday as that of Major Hollis from the 101st Airborne Division. A witness saw the pilot's glider break loose from a DC3's towrope and crash in Jorgen's field. Several neighbors rushed to the scene but the pilot was found dead. The fragile CG-4A glider the Americans are using to transport supplies and soldiers behind enemy lines was completely destroyed. No other soldiers were on board. The glider was being flown north as part of an allied plan to capture the Rhine Crossings. The plan appears to be succeeding. The United States' War Department has been notified.'

"My neighbor came and told me of a man who had dropped from the sky. That night I prayed for him. I prayed that he saw the stars as he fell. . . . I prayed for his family. I prayed for Alfons. I was not told till a week later that Alfons was killed in action that day." She blows on the surface of her tea, then sips. "Twenty years ago my daughter came home with a school project. She was to adopt an allied soldier's grave for Christmastime. I knew which grave it should be. And we continue.

"You are here now, Amy, because . . . ? Or am I asking a question too personal?"

I hesitate. "No one's come before, I think, because no one's wanted to bury him. But I think I need to."

Her cloudy hair moves with her nod.

"Will you continue, s'il vous plaît?" I ask. "I'll send money annually for—"

"No, no, I need this too. Here"—she reaches over and, her hands careful with the brittle pages, turns the scrapbook to another page—"See?"

An article the size of a large postage stamp floats against the black paper background on which it's pasted. She translates: "'Gustave Forret, manager of La Banque Nationale, was reported missing on 4 May, 1943. He was last seen boarding a train bound for Cambrai, France, at La Station de Louviere. If anyone has news of his whereabouts, please contact his wife, Ingrid Forret, care of the bank in Haine-St-Pierre.' They list the names of the others missing *aussi*. I won't read them." She sits back slowly.

"We never heard. Nothing about any of them. I don't know what it is about the body, *mon amie*. Just a shell. But we need that shell, to see it empty, for proof. It is that shell that allows us to manifest our love, and to ritualize our loss."

I search her face, try to read the hourglass lines between her brows and the creases that run vertically down her cheeks, and I see simply sad resignation, an expression I wish I had seen on my mother's face, even just once.

"Sometimes, when I am digging in the grave soil," she continues, "I think, maybe, somewhere, another person is doing the same for my father. . . . Let me know if you want something special. Here is my address." She gets up, finds pen and paper by a wall phone, and scribbles. "Don't lose it, *d'accord*? I want to keep connected."

"Oh, I have this picture of my father, from 1939. At least take this." I hand her my father's black-and-white Air Force Academy portrait, bordered by a white, serrated edge, that I carry in my wallet.

She smiles. "Your father's eyes. And the shape of his face. But you should keep this—"

"No, for some reason we have, like, twenty of those, and not many others."

"It will go in here." She places it on top of the scrapbook.

It's hard to relay the feeling of standing on a threshold and hugging a stranger so hard I can feel her small breasts and pointy bones, feel the shoulder blades that jut out like wings and the trail of vertebrae that are settling with age, feel the good life that is stored in her body. I inhale the scent that exudes from the crown of her head, a mixture of manmade shampoo and human musk. I want to inhale her whole spirit and take it with me, use her to push out the darkness that has resided in me my whole life. But I know only I can do the replacing.

When I leave, a light rain is beginning to blacken the slate walkway. I look up, up to the scudding clouds and to that place in the west. I am glad he fell here. My mother would not have taken such good care of him.

I awake once again to the cock's crow and the school bell chiming and the children's voices. Time passes differently here. Personal problems seem much smaller when juxtaposed against the evidence of a long stretch of human history and suffering. America is too new. We've lost sight of our place and our consequences.

I'm going home today, and it's OK. I pack up and wash, relieved to be going home to a long, luxurious shower and the lengthening hours of spring.

She anticipates the coming of snow and the dripping of melting ice that coats the scene as it did that winter she spent in Holland. That gray-green ice that rises with the dawn and reminds her of him, left behind. And in these new winter dreams, when she looks back, she runs to the window, now closed and barred (he was too pained and doomed to say good-bye). She returns to her party friends and dances alone but with abandon. She knows she will see the Bird Man again in another dream, half real, half spirit. She knows that he will never completely disappear.

HULDI

(INDIA, 1990)

Day 1, twilight

Surrounded by voices murmuring, laughing, and giggling as skin makes unaccustomed contact with her. She is the center of it all, sari radiating from her anointed body in iridescent petal folds. Women—relatives, friends, neighbors—hover about in a hum like honeybees eager to stroke and gather. What do they want? she wonders. What is that in their eyes? She is expected to be pale, fey, to keep her eyes modestly downcast, but she looks up through her lashes into Aunty's eyes. She is not sure, but thinks she sees a sadness or a weariness behind the dark-mirrored pupils. In an old neighbor's yellowing eyes she sees a craving, as if smoothing her preconnubial skin will smooth the neighbor's skin, bring something back to life. The handfuls of dough roll up her arms, calves, face, the aromatic oil hypnotizing. Resistant at first, coiling back at first, not used to being touched, she gradually gives in, tension draining. Someone is beating rhythmically on a drum; her heart begins to follow.

Day 2, dusk

She gives herself up more quickly. It is easier to play the timid bride-to-be tonight. She is leaving home in two days. Leaving Mama,

Papa, Sarita, and her dog, who barks at mountain lions and keeps
her awake at night. Leaving her room with its cot and dresser and
movie pictures pasted to the walls. Leaving the garden where she
reads, cosmos and marigolds from the States as bright as small
suns. Leaving to live at her in-laws' home, in a bedroom prepared
for her. She will be their obedient daughter. Someone is dancing
and singing. She opens her eyes. Everything is distant, fewer people
than yesterday. She watches tea and *laddus* being passed. They are
her favorite sweet, but she turns her head when Sarita puts one to
her lips. She looks at her own skin, and it is someone else's skin,
being smoothed and buffed and colored by the mustard oil and
turmeric she'd mixed into chickpea flour. Extra turmeric speeds up
the coloring process. Mama remarks on how fair her skin is
becoming. She hears the voice, but it is coming from far away.

Day 3, night

She gives herself up completely. The *mahandi* is painted onto her
hands and feet. The henna paste is green but will leave a red stain.
The swirls wind like snakes around her palms and fingers, up her
wrists. She likes the feel of the soft brush caressing her skin. A
place at the base of her spine tingles pleasantly. She will wash on
the morning of her wedding day. Wash away the green paste and
the layers of oil from three nights of *huldi*. The women leave and
Mama comes in, closing the curtain. Mama removes her sari,
petticoat, bodice. Rubs her whole body—her back, stomach, breasts,
thighs. Her match is outside in the garden, eating and drinking in
celebration. She is not to see him until tomorrow. His laugh floats
through the garden, along the strings of a Sitar, into her open
window. She closes her eyes, imagines that Mama's hands are his.

THE SIN EATER

M ost days, like this one, he lives like a snake coiled peacefully on a warm rock ledge down in the gorge, listening to the low groan of swollen frogs and the high-pitched buzz of flying insects. His home is the inward fold of rock that forms a cave overlooking the flat bed of what was once a mighty river. Now the river is narrowed into a shallow, bereft stream, clear in spring and muddy in summer.

This is how he wants it. No human cacophony disturbs his hard-won peace, though sometimes he hears the ghostly sobs and cries of the Indian lovers who leapt to their deaths from the high ridge above, or the subtle misery emanating from the crying logs and the acid wood of the chestnuts, killed by the blight. These voices he hears after the rain comes, dripping through branches that try to reach heaven, cleaving to the bark and running down into the dark, immortal soil. He likens this cleansing process to his own role, for he sees himself as rain, washing clean of guilt the minds of the living, as well as absolving the dead of their treachery and selfishness. And while the forests cannot sin, he hears their cries for the sins done to them, and for the sins they have witnessed amongst their clearings and glens. The logs screech near Bear Creek where ten Indians were treed like possums and shot down to earth. On Jessup Mountain, the pines cry, as the first unwitting Tree must have, the few witnesses left to view their foundations worn to a moonscape of gray soil and gullies carved from the logs skid by slave mules down the mountains' backs.

So even here he cannot completely escape from man's sin, but it is hard for him to leave himself and his people behind absolutely—dependency, he has learned, makes vast allowances for sin.

A sourwood tree grows from the rock outcrop above his cave. Today he rouses himself from his meditative slumber and climbs up to hack off a branch. He is careful to trim only a part that is growing unwieldy. Although it is bad luck to burn it as fuel, he gets many things from the sourwood. The leaves serve as a thirst quencher when his stream turns to mud; the bark, when boiled with yellow root and moonshine whiskey, makes a strong stomach medicine; the flowers perfume his memories. He thinks they look like angels' fingers—pale, white, slender. Today he takes the flowering branch up the natural rock stairs, along the ridge to Crow Hill and into a circle of red maple. Here is where he lays down the angel fingers, on a mossy mound at the copse's center, and throws away a palmful of wilted white daisies.

Long ago, as far back as his memory can stretch, there was a little, sweet child—"Letty," he murmurs—his companion in childhood. Even when he was young, still a part of the community, he had a need to escape his reality. He was not content to let Letty just "happen," an ordinary event like all others. He carefully constructed a vision that fairies had left her to be found in a dewy wildflower by her mother's front stoop. He found her hair to be slippery soft as the silken tassel of corn when he eventually dared to touch it. And she was always untouched—by grime, sickness, bad feeling—unlike the other mountain children. The scent from her skin was as heady and filling as wild roses at dusk, and her eyes were deep with wild wisdom. It was she who taught him to love the mountains.

He has an early memory of her mother laundering, stirring the big boiling cauldron. To keep her curious Letty from wandering too close, she sat her daughter down under a tree, painted molasses on both of her hands, gave her a freshly dropped owl feather. Letty would spend many quiet hours with that owl feather, examining its detail and moving it from one sticky hand to the other. She never once screamed in frustration, unable to shake it off, as he surely would have.

He thinks maybe such a soul was destined to leave early. Their marriage during her fifteenth harvest season never came to pass. Letty borrowed milk from a neighbor one balmy summer day, after which the neighbor's only fly-bitten cow dried up. Letty was branded Witch with frightening speed. For of course, Mother McBride reminded everyone, if you take something from someone you have a power over them. It was Letty who killed the cow. What, or who, might follow? To the jealous and coveting villagers, it all fit so conveniently—her uncommon beauty, her way with birds and small creatures.

They came for her before the rain, when the leaves bent their backs to the wind. She and her parents had no chance against the rage of the entire community, no chance to survive their surge of justice. And certainly no chance to survive the water test. She was bound and gagged, dumped into Walker's Pond. If she sank, she was innocent—if she bobbed to the surface, held aloft by her demonic powers, she was guilty.

His sweetheart could not even struggle. She was pulled down into the muck and dirge of the stagnant water, which filled her body and took her life before anyone would save her. He still has the horizontal scars across his upper arms and around his wrists, from being bound to a nearby tree, from the effort of trying to break free.

He now sees sin in everything and casts stones readily. For he watched God-fearing neighbors stand in dark judgment along the muddy shore, watched the faces contort in hate, watched children clap and laugh.

He knows he is not without sin, either. His sin is that he can never forgive, never accept.

Crow Hill is just close enough to the village's center to have the low sound of a bell tolling brought to his ears. He raises his bowed head from the grave and counts. Fifty-six. That would be Uncle Joshua, ailing for months now. He knows they will soon come for the Sin Eater.

He goes about his business, waiting for the sign. The evening is still and crickets play their wings in frantic succession. At the head of the stream, trickling from mountain rock, he takes pleasure in gathering wild greens. Up on the ridge of the gorge he finds peppergrass and meadow onion. Paradise is always here, he tells himself many times. And more than thinking it, he feels it, deeply, believing the men he knows mythologize and ignore Paradise, all around them, as an excuse to destroy.

Back on his ledge he prepares his meal. Above, the sky fades to show the half-moon, its tips pointing down. He reads this fact as a foreshadowing of rain to come.

They will now be setting up with the body, Uncle Joshua lovingly washed and prepared for heaven—because no one ever prepares a body for hell. A neighbor, Lucas probably, will be hammering the casket together. The night is hotter than the day was. They must make speed in this weather, though the rain will bring some relief.

He finds the silver dollar where he expects it, in a natural indentation in a granite boulder at the top of the gorge. Beneath it is a scrap of brown paper bag with the name "J. O'Toole" scrawled in dark, heavy pencil. He is right. Joshua O'Toole, once leader to a rough gang of moonshiners, is being buried today, despite the showers that pass overhead, so quickly that they sound like the wind in the trees.

He knows the townspeople he turned his back on through memory and one person—Jim Gregor, the booger man. Gregor is also an outsider, an articulate beggar who trades his haunting tales for a meal and a place to sleep. Gregor knows everything—who's pregnant, who's sick, who's sinning. Sometimes Gregor comes to warn him that so-and-so is dying. So he waits for the church bell to toll the age, and he knows. Gregor also brings him the few supplies he needs—cloth, thread, needles, tools, kerosene, whiskey. Gregor was second cousin to Letty.

He knows how to walk without disturbing the undergrowth. He approaches the O'Toole farm from the west, the wooded side, always looking for concealment. A canvas is stretched on poles over a patch of grass, the casket beneath, out of the rain. The town gathers under the outer fringes, solemn and black as the clouds scudding overhead. The women are forward, the men let the rain fall on their hats and shoulders.

He cannot watch a funeral without morbid thoughts of Letty intruding. He sees once again her mother, face pinched so hard, massaging her daughter's marble-white cheeks in order to close the terrified eyes. He hands her mother the silver nickel coins to keep them shut. He listens quietly, as the women decide to dress her in white, like a child, like a sacrifice. He begs Letty's uncle to make the coffin, for few want to be involved, and he himself smoothes up a rock for her grave. He insists they bury her in a spot far away from the traitorous parishioners, and they bury her with asters and an owl feather within her crossed palms. Ashes to ashes, dust to dust, sleep well . . .

The time has come for him to step from the bushes, bathed in the green light of sin. He creeps forward to the rough casket, shiny from black oil. The crowd shrinks from his appearance as much as from threat of contamination. He plays his part of Sin Eater, unkempt beard and hair, unpatched clothes, unwashed skin—for everyone expects sin to appear in such form. He in turn shrinks from their disdain, but reaches for the apple and slice of black bread and hard cheese that rests atop the casket, on top of the sinner who rests beneath. He takes a bite from the apple, the small noise a firecracker in the expectant silence. A collective sigh follows—their neighbor is now free from sin, it has been taken in and devoured by another who is a savior, yet a demon by his very act of saving. Unlike the Faith Healers who blow the breath of faith into their subjects, he inhales and digests their fears and follies and greater acts of violence.

He retreats back to the protective arms of the woods, finishes his meal. When the warm rain passes, he goes in search of mushrooms, where the dark blue violets bloom beneath old, hoary apple trees. He thinks he hears a sound like a woman crying— perhaps it is an early screech owl.

He is not bitter that the accumulation of his fellow man's deepest secrets makes him the blackest sinner of all, that there might be no one to take on his sins when he passes. After all, despite the hate that sometimes threatens to engulf him, what he, the Sin Eater does, is finally a most desperate, sacrificial act of love.

MEMSAHIB

⁓

Summers in my village, nestled in India's Himalayan foothills, are not as oppressive as those further south. That is why during this country's colonial days, the British, fleeing the unfamiliar, ovenlike heat of the plains during the hotter months, made these northern villages into hill stations for their summer homes.

As a child, I remember catching whisperings of discontent regarding the foreign neighbors. Usually they came from Uncle, spitting remarks on "cantonment" around the hookah stem clenched between his teeth. Too young to understand the malice in his voice, I could only take the word by its definition: Colonizers take hold of the land—in our village it was Granite Hill—and in their Imperial way strip and clear it as a foundation for their Western-style homes and military offices. Just outside our village, they were close enough to keep a vigilant eye on us, yet far enough away to avoid becoming too familiar.

My friends and I spied on their cantonment from behind the safety of the thick pine trunks that grew from the back of the hill, and wondered why these "visitors" got to live in such orderly, sparkling, white-washed places, while we, who belonged to the land

and forests and meadows, had to remain in stone structures and cottages that were mostly dirt-colored and full of holes and unelectrified darkness.

But that was my only negative thought about the colonial relationship, just a glimmering, really, besides being resentful that the military had taken over our playing field for their military games. And clean new bungalows rearing up from recently scarred earth was all I envisioned when I heard "cantonment." So when I caught sight of the Bari Memsahib—the first white woman I had ever seen outside of a Tarzan movie—she was not the state governor's wife but a maharani, a queen, pale skin like a goddess, gracing our small village. For only a queen would be preceded by a retinue of attendant scouts, be surrounded by four stiff guards in blinding white tunics and turbans, draped in royal red cloth, emblazoned with lotuses in fine gold thread and little hand-cut mirrors, belted at the waist. Such color and display of wealth attracted a band of followers, mostly children.

When the weather was fair, and the early morning or late afternoon light left slanting shadows, she walked from the cantonment, guards at right angles to her, never varying their distance, four corners to her, the center. We did not recognize them, and concluded amongst ourselves that they came with the military entourage from Delhi.

Memsahib was not as splendidly dressed as were they, but authority resonated from her raised arm and extended to the height of her steady parasol. My memory of what she wore is weak—a blur of feminine skirts, shawls, boots—but that ruffled parasol was the untouched white of the mansion from which she emerged. Her face, pale and translucent as alabaster, shadowed and serious with a mission, was impervious to the dusty, staring crowd.

I could never see into her eyes. The guards kept us at a proper distance. "*Nazdik matjao*, don't get too close," they snapped at anyone who dared step into the royal circumference. What I could see was a mouth bright with lipstick. I had never seen lips so red.

When she stopped in her approach to the village center, we stopped and waited while she tilted her head and prospected the view. I also tilted my head and looked where she did, trying to glean what was so special about this wall, or that yard. I could never anticipate where she would stop. She picked the strangest places to set her slatted seat and prop her large canvas—usually a corner or sidewalk facing the old part of Rajkor. As onlookers, we looked at each other, amused, but of course we tried to hide our amusement out of respect.

This was the moment her band of followers fell away. But I remained, my imagination captured, staring hard at the streets and roofs, paved and shingled with slate quarried from nearby, at the stone buildings, walls crumbling in places, and at the painted woodwork framing them, peeling and blistering under hot sun.

"*Hatto!* Move away!" a guard cautioned me once. I had unconsciously been shifting toward her in the road dust, drawn to one particular painting I can still see, could even paint myself if I so wished. Memsahib's face remained calm, absorbed, the quiet expression of the artist under the spell of creation unbroken by my transgression. Her knife was putting finishing touches to her vision of the scene before us—the sweet shop in early morning, the white sun, not yet risen to its noon pitch, in the eastern part of the sky casting the doorway and window beneath turquoise-striped awnings in strokes of flat black shade. Gray-pink was dabbed onto the sun-bleached walls, remains of an undercoat of bright pink, of an edict ten years prior to paint the entire village pink.

Much time was spent on the outside, on the wandering, nameless *sadhu* who decided that for today, this was where he would rest. She found the right color to paint the round copper begging bowl, lying in the curve of his wrinkled arm. A pale suggestion of a pai dog slept in a horizontal stroke in the shade. Flies buzzed around both sleepers, but she didn't add those. Brown hens, pecking around the doorway, added spots of burnt sienna and brown madder.

"*Hatto!*" It was not until the guard's cry that I realized my feet had brought me too close. I was pulled forward by the painted scene, so ready for me to enter. I belonged there, both inside the undeveloped shop darkness and outside in the branding sun.

And at that moment, the voice of warning—"*Hatto!*"—still resonating in the crisp air, I understood and felt, in a child's limited yet full way, the divide. She belonged where she was, on the outside looking in, the observer making her statement on the provincial scene framed with her colonial mind-set.

I wanted her to recognize my anger, to see me in my newfound awareness, my loss of innocence about her people. She simply continued to raise her knife, to caress the scene into being. If it weren't for the guards, I would have thrown a rock at the easel. Her imperviousness now felt like the final insult. I turned away, the parasol the last thing my eye took in, knowing I would not come again.

Indian independence arrived, finally, the following August of '47. We settled down in the front room to listen to All India Radio, my brothers and sisters on cushions on the floor, the adults on chairs and daises. With great gusto, Uncle refilled the clay bowl of the hookah with his most fragrant tobacco. "This is a fine day for Rajkor. A fine, auspicious day for India. I am glad to be alive on such a day." The family agreed. We tuned in to the more elegant words of Nehru, his voice broadcast all across the world: "At the stroke of the midnight hour, when the world sleeps, India will awake to life and freedom . . . when we step out from the old to the new, when an age ends, and when the soul of a nation, long suppressed, finds utterance."

Of course we did not sleep that night. We took to the streets, a nation's long-held breath being released in a torrent of ecstatic laughter and chatter and a need to touch our friends and neighbors, as if to acknowledge in the physical gesture that we had survived, were still present as ourselves. We climbed walls and trees, shook branches and screeched out our triumph. When the Indian flag was hoisted to the rhythm of the church bell announcing midnight, a collective cheer took up that must have echoed off the hillsides till it reached Nepal.

Rajkor rejoiced for days with fireworks and festivals when the British, along with the state governor, left. His wife had stopped painting our village, had probably returned to Britain for safety months prior. I didn't join the crowd that went to jeer at the governor's exit, though through some pine trees I caught sight of his black car as it tore down the road below my house, car flag waving its Union Jack viciously from the hood.

Refugees in our own bruised land, we salvaged our traditions and culture, but never were they the same again, and nothing from then on would be completely our own.

Today, the memsahib is more than memory. She is part of the landscape of my mind as well as an old fixture in an environment as colorful as was she. And fifty years later, on this anniversary of our independence, my anger is reduced by the soporific of passing time. I pause from the scene I paint—of mountains, of a Hindu temple, of a stream or valley—and take pleasure in the expression I feel resting on my face, that same, other-worldly, absorbing expression of the artist with whom I am now able to acknowledge a bond. Some things, such as our commonalities, should never be denied or repressed. They are what keep us connected, yet independent.

Above the cot where Uncle spends his final days, fingering his bed sheets, hangs one of her early landscapes, salvaged after the exodus. His eyes, while open, continually search the impressionistic vista of Granite Hill for his own meaning. I, in turn, search for my own.

SUSPENDED

—

*I*t can be exuberance or anger or fear that makes people drive too fast. In this case it is anger that rockets her Pontiac to breakneck speed against the barrier of darkness, rather than the usual gradual silken entry of metal and air that pushes the dark aside and leaves it behind. Then, in one of those moments that escapes the careful assumptions of the unconscious, something that should not be there is there—a creature's round, panicked eye rolled back, four legs in frenetic motion desperate for survival sailing across her vision and the hood. She is losing control, the rear wheels slipping across the yellow line, taking on their own power and sending her flying off the road, into the limbs of an evergreen that roots below the macadam edge. The old tree somehow knows to hold her just so, and when she focuses again, she finds her car is suspended, engine taking her nowhere. No movement in her pinned arms or legs, but she can move her neck to the side. She is alive. At least, she feels she is, for she cannot believe this is the afterlife, and she doesn't think she merits purgatory. Though it begins to feel like a place of limbo, as the sounds of traffic from the old route above gain and fade with the sun's strength. She cannot honk or

117

reach her cell when it begins to ring, over and over. And the engine sputters to a final halt, and the phone battery, along with her unanswered screams, loses strength. The vehicle becomes a cold shell, the windows glazed with the fog of her breath. She licks the damp driver's window to survive, takes back her own exhalations and the sweat of frustration and fright. Yet beads form again to trail down and nourish her. Sometimes, the spring winds batter her window and tongue, and the limbs sway and creak, so she sends her mind up above the tree line where she will keep it if gravity wins and the tree grows weary. But the tree loves her too much to drop her and she loves the tree, the window, and the rain that drips over the visor to her waiting mouth. Then when the sun rises on the seventh day, there is noise below and something like a human face behind the glazed window and a voice promising safety, asking her if she knows what day it is. She says yes, it's the greatest day of my life, and she means it, but still she cries in grief when they have to chainsaw through a heavy limb to release her.

THE BURNINGS

I work hard in the dormant month of February to remind myself of the warmth and life and light all being stored up in the surrounding woods and earth and animals. But this February I am interrupted by the exit of one life.

I watch, from my bay window, cardinals forage for seed in the brown grass beneath the shepherd's crook. The brilliant-feathered male pushes the female away. She hops back at a respectful distance, unperturbed, I think. She must know that in just a few months her mate will once again be feeding her in courtship.

When Lenore first comes into the living room to tuck a knitted afghan around my arthritic knees, I don't see she is crying. Then a small catch of her breath takes me away from the scene outside.

"Ethel called . . . Linda is gone."

"Gone?"

Lenore backs up without looking behind until she reaches the couch, then falls into it. "A few days ago. Liver disease. She kept it a secret, how bad she was. The funeral's tomorrow."

I've noticed, in recent years, that the tears on my wife's good face no longer fall—they meander through the creases, find rest in

119

flat rivulets that begin at her eyes, eyes of a blue no longer intense but soft and comforting.

"Do ya hear me, Donald?" she asks after a silence I know she judges to be too long.

"I hear you." When my wife gets upset, her brogue grows stronger.

The cardinals fly off in unison when the sudden turn of my head in the window reflection startles them. Or maybe it is Judith, my neighbor to the right, crossing the tree-line of white pines, plastic container in hand.

"Damn it, Lenore, she's doing it again—taking my seed!"

Judith tilts the tube feeder and gathers the millet and sunflower seed mixture into her container, then takes small, guilty, elfin steps back to her property.

The afghan slides to the floor. "I'm calling her this time. She's emptied half the feeder!"

Lenore sighs, wipes her face first with her fingertips, then with the backs of her hands. "Just let it be, Donald, just let *her* be."

I wait by the car for my wife to check the stove and leave the house. The winter sky looks vast, a gray ocean. I reach to the car for ballast—a touch of vertigo for a moment, a feeling of insignificance.

We are becoming used to late-night phone calls and the sad, necessary flurry of funeral preparations. But this time, the death of our friend and neighbor's daughter, Linda, hits harder. A life not fully lived, both in years and accomplishments, is harder to celebrate.

I can't help but think about my own daughter, who used to play with Linda in a tree house her father and I erected in the woods between our two properties. If Melissa had just left me now, forever, I would never look at the world as whole again. It would always be a treacherous puzzle, with the most important piece missing. Lenore would feel the same—she had immediately rushed to the phone to call Melissa, ostensibly to tell her the news, but I knew the mother needed to affirm that the daughter hadn't somehow disappeared, too.

The North Parish church lot is crowded with mourners. We are directed to the last row of seats, handed programs for the service.

"Her ex-husband is giving the eulogy," Lenore whispers.

I glance at the name she points to, printed in uneven typewriter font. "They divorced, what, ten years ago?"

"He's over there."

But I'm looking to my friend, Rowan, in the first row. I hear some heavy words like "pain" and "alcoholism" during the service, and move to escape the church's old, overactive heaters.

The ground outside is uneven, frost-heaved. The stones that frame the church are large, chiseled granite taken from parish land. They have been hewn into a strong, seemingly sturdy house of worship. I study the dry moss and ochre-tinged lichen that discolors the mortar, which cements the rocks that will outlast all of those they house.

Lenore returns from her lunch with that cold, sweet smell of winter air about her. I'm fixing a barley stew for dinner, and it has to bake in the oven for several hours. I ease a knife into a mushroom, slice it in half.

Lenore puts a carrot piece into her mouth and chews carefully. "That was hard. Ethel cried a lot, but I think she needed to."

"Where did you go?"

"Palmers. We didn't really eat, but it looked good . . . soup and salad."

"We're having stew tonight."

"Thanks. . . . Donald?"

"Hmmm?"

"You should talk to Rowan. Ethel says he won't talk to her. She thought maybe, you being a man, and a friend—"

"Oh, hon, what would I say?"

"Don't say anything. Listen."

I point to the red cooking wine next to the stove. She hands it to me so I can pour it into the simmering pot.

"What if he doesn't talk? Doesn't want to? Sometimes talk makes things worse."

Lenore puts her fists on her hips, elbows out—as she does when she's frustrated with me—and shakes her head slowly.

"Donald MacIntyre. Just be a good friend, okay? He's gonna do some burnin' tomorrow, you go see him."

"I've got nothing left to burn this season."

"Then *make* somethin' ta burn," she snaps, as chilly as the evening that's coming on.

The cozy smell of a wood fire wends its way down from the hill above our land. Pushed by a bone-chilling wind, it enters the cracks around my old, four-paned windows. Lenore comes into the living room a second time, stares at me in an effort to get me moving.

I put down the book I've been pretending to read for several hours, unable to concentrate on the gardening tool chapter.

"I'll go, I'll go."

I gear up for the cold, pull on a knit cap, and set out into the backyard to find something to burn.

I find the end-of-winter landscape so unalluring. The cold covers all natural scents, and life contracts into itself, waiting, biding its time. The sounds of animal calls still hold, though: the murder of crows that caw when they see me, their sharp eyes looking to my hands for the whiteness of stale bread; the nattering of alarmed squirrels, amidst creaking limbs; the scream of a red-tailed hawk, and the cacophony of the crows now in pursuit.

Nature, I think, has a temper. Last night it was angry, lashing about. Some old oak branches were thrown to the ground, both black with rot and white with fungus. One lies stuck, like a broken arm, having plunged end first into our lawn. Still, they are not enough to burn.

My eyes fall on the picnic bench sitting patiently under the pines, the trees lacy from the loss of needles. The bench leans to the left, its surface seamed and weathered like silver driftwood. In summertime you'll see moss growing in cracks, and little red fungus that looks like tiny, haphazard bunches of "lollipop trees," as Melissa calls them.

Without hesitation, I unlock the tool shed and pull out the axe. I hit hard, taking time to rest during the slow, steady attack.

The red wheelbarrow squeaks through the dry, shrunken undergrowth. I push it over scrub and dormant vines of wild strawberry, sumac, and deadly nightshade. Rowan and I have slowed in our quest to keep the woods between our homes clear of the kinds of small, weedy greenery that impedes progress. His side is especially overgrown since he began summering in Maine—front lawn overtaken by myrtle, rhododendrons, tall grasses, and towering pines. I force the barrow through the trees, aiming for the hot orange light flashing between trunks.

He looks up when I enter the clearing, his eyes hidden behind glasses that reflect his bonfire. The two round, flickering globes hide his expression. He is in a circle of cardboard boxes and green trash bags.

"Smelled the burning, had this old picnic table to get rid of." I begin to feed the flames with the old cedar axed into three-foot sections. The fire embraces the wood, sucks out what's left of its life like a vampire, and tosses its ash to the sky. While I say a silent farewell to the bench that once supported my family during picnics, absorbed our beer and wine and lemonade, Rowan carefully, gently, gives the fire what I soon realize are letters—papers of different colors, faded pinks and yellows, colors of our daughters' youths, those boldly drawn daisies and perfect round dots of the sixties and early seventies decorating some of them. They all burn the same way—corners to center.

He opens one envelope, a plain white one, pulls out the yellow, legal-size paper, and reads to himself. "It's from me," he says. "It's a letter I wrote to her after her divorce, asking her to get help." He raises his right thumb and forefinger to his glasses, efficiently wipes away the tears gathering in the corners.

"I have to go through all her stuff now. Ethel can't do it. Her clothes I took down to the Salvation Army. I took her books to the library. But what do I do with these personal things? So much paper . . . I can't watch the garbage truck take them away."

He slides the letter back into its envelope, hesitates for a moment, then drops it into the fire. The flames feed off wood and paper, growing hotter, forcing us back. Fire is so fascinating because it looks alive. It almost speaks to me. Mesmerized, I stare. I hear flames, loud as thunder, screams.

Cautiously, I remember. "I used to live in New York, before my folks moved to Haverhill." I pause, letting my mind refill with long-buried memories and feelings. "You remember May 6, 1937? Also my birthday. I'd finally gotten that BB gun from Hammond's storefront window. And I remember it was a gray day, storming over New Jersey. I was out playing with my gun, and suddenly there was this, this silver balloon on the horizon, growing larger and larger. It passes over the Newson farm. I see ribbed sides . . . huge, black-and-white swastikas in a red square, flag flying from the tail . . . mooring ropes curving down from its nose. The hum of engines is really loud. It passes overhead, this *huge*, stately bird. It covers my view of the sky. I take aim . . . *Bam!*"

"You shot at the *Hindenberg*?" Rowan is listening, his hands in his front jacket pockets. I bring my arms back down from their frozen, raised position.

"I heard the broadcast on Dad's Gabriel Heater radio that night. The announcer's voice broke. Sounds of death and disaster. *My* disaster. I killed those people, I thought. . . . I buried my BB gun; lived, years, with my secret. It was only when I got old enough to know a BB couldn't reach that far that I could accept not being responsible. Can you believe that, though? I really thought I was responsible."

Rowan's mouth shows the crack of a smile, like light under a door. He shakes his head. "You stupid son-of-a-bitch."

I stay with Rowan awhile longer. We empty boxes and bags together, as ceremoniously as possible. The last paper is tossed, and he shakes his head again, slaps me on the back. I hear something released in his laugh, and the sound, like an animal cry, goes up into the trees and gets caught and tossed around in their outreaching, comforting limbs.

TURTLE HUNTING

H e took me turtle hunting once. How many of you can say that your lovers have taken you turtle hunting?

We ask for sensitivity, but eventually their pain becomes more than we can bear.

I'll take you, he says. Maybe we'll find one.

And he pulls me through the trees, green-yellow dappling the spongy floor. We pause by granite slabs, tilted sideways to the earth, crimson ivy pulling them down. And we stand silently, our shadows falling over the dark stones.

We were intruders foreshadowing our own demise.

I try to read the chiseled names and dates eroded by lichen. Their names did not even last a century.

The turtles are by the water, he says. You can see their small nostrils sometimes, just above the surface.

We walk by the edge, and I try to share his wonder, try to ignore the swamp mud tugging at my white sneakers. I wipe them off on damp leaves of skunk cabbage when his back is turned. And I try not to mind the flame-colored poison ivy. I think of the turtles, their bodies sealed off from the world, breathing the only reason for them to stay in it.

They have survived millions of years, their reward for knowing the right balance between vulnerability and defense.

He gives up after a few hours, unsuccessful.

We want what does not exist.

What do you want to do now? Go home? he asks.
    We return the way we thought we had come, but a sea of tall grass arrests our progress. Surrounded by grasshoppers, gossamer wings, he takes my hand.
    This is the perfect place to make love, he says.

What must remain in order for us to be able to say that we have survived?

I turn my head, my sorrow one with the swarm of miniscule insects I slap away.

DELIGHT

—

> "In this great auditorium under the sky,
> all of us are free." —Harold Ickes

This is how Delight wakes up every morning—the neighbor's bantam begins his guttural crowing, and the wild blackbirds in the palm trees outside her window start their caterwauling. It is like coming out of a place of deep, smooth darkness into a light growing stronger through the opening and closing of many unoiled, rusty metal doors.

Monday / *lunes*

The first day of the workweek, she makes the confection that lasts longest. She boils pure cane sugar in a large vat, adding glucose, red food coloring, and strawberry extract. Just after she turns down the burner to keep the mix from scalding, she adds sesame seeds that will float in the lollipop like schools of white reef fish. The mixture hardens in small cylindrical molds around the plastic straws she inserts for handles. When they are solid, she puts them in small clear bags and ties green ribbon around the stems.

Her candy shop is up the steep hill from her home. By 7 a.m., she is unlocking the wrought iron gates that protect her windows and front door from invasion. It's March, and the ocean waves today were predicted by the local surf shop to be four feet high. So a group of surfers is eagerly assembled, ready to grab and carry away some coffee, sodas, beer, and bags of nachos and chips she keeps stocked.

From everywhere in the world these men, and a few women, come to her beach town in Puerto Rico. To her, they appear to be the same—toned, with evenly burnished copper tans, suits tied loose, hair on the men either shaved or in locks. All looking for the perfect wave and a free ride. They flirt with her shop assistant, Mercedes, who barely reaches Delight's shoulder, even when her dark hair is teased up.

They never look directly at Delight, whose neck is permanently bent, from birth, to her left. She is like a coconut palm that stretches way over a spot of sand to reach more sun. They avoid the awkwardness of looking at imperfection from their own well-formed frames, and gravitate to the one who is safe to look at.

The local boys know her and chat. Some have tried to take advantage of her difference, assuming it was a free pass. One boy, Ramon, tried to physically straighten her neck while they were seated in the front of his Jeep. A small scar now runs white down his right cheek, in the shape of a sickle blade. He holds no grudge, however.

Delight pours coffee for a tall man with a black eye, while his shorter friend stacks four six-packs on the counter of cold Medalla. Mercedes bags them while Delight rings up the purchase. The short one tells the tall one he has been drinking since he got up. Delight is glad to see them leave.

She realizes, as the shop quiets down, that someone has been waiting patiently in the back corner. He steps forward and up to the counter, smiling right at her. She returns his gaze but doesn't lift her practical mouth. "Sorry for my fellow Americans. Some of us get real irritating at times."

She is not used to surfers from off-Island talking to her without any eye deviation. Her core body heat rises with the internal dilemma of how to respond. Mercedes steps in. "Can I get you anything?"

He orders black coffee and gathers several bottles of water from the cold case, then examines the confections under the glass counter, cloudy from scratches and fingerprints. "Who makes these?"

"Delight does," Mercedes answers, nodding in her direction. Delight hopes the sweat forming on her brow and upper lip is not noticeable under the fluorescence.

"That so? I'll take one of the . . . what is that called?"

"A *pilón*, a pop."

"Yeah, one of those."

He unwraps it. Delight, pretending to wipe down the counter with a rag, watches him as he leaves the store with it in his mouth, the stick out to the side like a cigarette. Through the linear spaces between the signage on the window, she follows his muscled back as it makes its way to a rental car with a board strapped on top. No one else is in the car.

She imagines him surfing with the pop still sticking from his mouth.

Tuesday / *martes*

The second day is set aside for *dulce de ajonjolí*, the sesame seed confection that is a descendant of the Spanish nougat. It is her biggest seller, and she takes special orders for it around the holidays.

First, she coats metal trays with peanut oil. Then, with two pans on the stove, she toasts the seeds and melts sugar and honey, combining the two with a wooden spoon worn down by generations of candymakers. The mixture is then poured in the pans, topped with wax paper, rolled to about ¼-inch thick, and then cut into one-inch squares. When mostly cooled, she packs them in boxes.

As she prepares to leave for the store, she hears footsteps, and the kitchen curtain is parted. The material is pushed aside by her father, one hand scratching his balding head, the other on his stomach, which protrudes from a gray undershirt. "Alegría, *café* . . . *huevos frito*."

Delight has to drop what she is doing, grind the coffee beans, and fry two eggs. "How was the cockfight last night?"

"*¡Carajo!* I lost all my money on one lame *gallo*. Only good for doing *¡quiquiriquí!* " It is the answer she is most often given, and why she is grateful to her *abuelita* for teaching her how to support herself. *"Nieta,"* her grandmother once said, putting a stool next to the stove for her little granddaughter to stand on and peer sideways at her kitchen magic, "you may never have a man in your life who will take care of you. You must learn to take care of yourself. I will teach you how." And the crooked girl watched the transformation of many common parts mix and boil and melt into a perfect confection.

She is late to the store, but Mercedes has opened it with her extra key and is already serving customers. Rushing, Delight walks past the surfer who had spoken to her the previous day. Only after she is in her place behind the counter does she look up and realize he has said good morning and she has not responded. He is still smiling, aware she is preoccupied.

"Oh, yes, I am sorry, sir, *buenos días.* What can we get you today?"

"What's in your boxes?"

She opens one; the aroma of roasted sesame and dark honey rises up. "Sesame candy, very popular here. Tourists take it home as gifts."

"Then I'll take a whole box."

Delight keeps her decorating material in the back of the store. She cuts blue and yellow ribbon and ties it around the white box, curling the ribbon ends. It is hot, and she feels herself getting hotter again, her pulse beating faster. She lifts the hem of her cotton shirt and wipes her forehead before returning to the front.

His eyebrows are blond, lighter than his toffee-colored hair. They lift slightly when he sees the fancy box. "Thanks." He doesn't leave. When a customer comes in and Mercedes is distracted, he leans over the counter, smelling of coconut sun block, and asks Delight, "Will you go to a concert at the plaza with me tonight?"

The heat returns in waves and moves up from her center to her face where she knows she can't hide it. She blushes even more, knowing she is blushing. "Uhhh . . ." She has no reason to say no.

"I'll take that as a yes. Pick you up around eight? Can I have your number?"

Feeling oddly at ease now, Delight lets him know that she doesn't have a phone, but that eight works fine. She writes her address on a paper napkin, which he takes and folds carefully in half, tucking it under the center of the box where the ribbon gathers.

Delight is floating. He is holding her hand, guiding her through the crowded plaza. She knows many of the concert-goers, and she sees different expressions cross their faces as they pass. Some frown, some smile. She tries to hold her head as straight as she can as the band plays a jazzy number. At the edge of the green, a foursome of local men play dominoes at a card table.

"See the man on the right?" she says to the surfer holding her hand. Marcus. His name she found out is Marcus Shield. He is so close, she can feel his golden arm hairs feathering hers. Bending his head to hear her better, his chin-length locks brush her cheek. Her cheek feels electrified. "He lost his Chevy Bel Air to the man on the left last year, playing that game."

Marcus shakes his head. "Can't imagine needing to win so much at a game that I'd lose that much."

"But you gamble your life when you surf, *sí*?"

"I'm more careful than some. I don't ride a wave I'm not familiar with. I want to live to ride again. So, no, Delight, I don't gamble my life." He pauses and laughs. "Maybe a tooth or a broken finger, but not my life."

She senses this is true, why he seems different from the other surfers that pass through. She knows, too, that she is a wave to him, and he is waiting for the right moment.

Wednesday / *miércoles*

Delight has trouble waking to the birds' metallic screeching. The bedding is soft, luscious, and she wants to stay in it, reliving last night. But she has to start the *besitos de coco*.

In a dream state, she pours grated coconut into water, brings it to a boil, and stirs in brown sugar. She reduces the heat, stirs till it thickens, then drops the spoonfuls of coconut onto cookie sheets. On one sheet she drizzles dark, melted chocolate over the mounds in serpentine patterns. No time for the chocolate to dry today, she packs the kisses away, much in the same way she packed away into her memory the brief kisses in the car last night. Just a few soft ones, gentle, salty, him bending in her direction, with a final kiss on her brow, like a benediction.

She came home last night to her father passed out on the couch, his wooden saints scattered around him in various states of creation.

Marcus is outside, leaning, his eyes behind sunglasses and his face pointed up to catch the early-morning sun that is fighting through the clouds. His red rash guard pops out against the green, pocked, concrete building. Hearing her approach, he looks down over the tops of his shades. "Here, I'll take those." And he takes the boxes of kisses from her while she opens the store, key hand shaking. She wanted him to be here, but had steeled herself for disappointment.

"The waves aren't going to be good today. How 'bout I help out here till you get off, then we can do something?"

Mercedes' mouth forms into a small round O when she walks in a few minutes later and sees him behind the counter. Delight catches the grin that passes between her and Marcus. Without saying anything, with just a nod, Mercedes joins them behind the counter. The surfers begin to drift in, planning their beverages and snacks for a different kind of day.

When the last coconut kiss is sold and no customer appears for an hour, Delight closes up early. Mercedes is happy enough to leave with her boyfriend, who shows up in a faded Datsun.

Of course Marcus wants to pull Delight to the beach, but she doesn't know how to swim. Has no bathing suit. "Just put on some dark shorts and a halter top."

Delight doesn't own a halter, either, just bras, the large and practical kind. She picks out a brown one that looks somewhat like a bathing top, and covers it with a pink T-shirt.

Marcus is on the living room couch when she comes out of her room. She feels a sense of intimacy that she has never shared before. A man is in her house while she is changing, and she feels safe. The smell of cedar wood rises up from the worn cushions as he sifts around a pile of wood shavings her father hadn't bothered to clean up. He holds an unfinished statue that must have been started that morning. The eight-inch image of a frocked man with arms raised, palms forward, eyes closed and mouth frozen in prayer, still waits for plaster and colorful paint. But she likes the statues best now, in their natural, simple state.

"My father is a *santero.* He makes saints for the souvenir shops and sells them on the highway. He is probably out there now, trying to make *dinero* for the cockfight tonight." And if he doesn't, Delight thinks to herself, he'll look around the house and try to find where I hid it this time.

"It's beautiful. I'd like to meet him."

Delight pauses at the front door. "No. My father, he carves the *santos,* but he does not lead a *vida santa,* how you say it? . . . saintly life?"

"I should still meet him, Delight. Shouldn't I?"

She looks at Marcus, standing before her, the wooden image still in his hand. For the first time, he seems unconfident, questioning. What does he want from her? she wonders. How far is he planning on taking this? He leaves in three days.

All she can do is shrug, and ask him to return the statue as he found it.

Delight is flying. On blue-green waves that race to the shore, supporting her as she clings to the surfboard Marcus releases. It is pure, just a few seconds of nothing more than a lifting, breathless sensation. She falls off the board and into the sandy shallows, struggles to stand in the reverse drag, and grins at Marcus who has taken in the next wave, using his body as a board.

"*Más*," she says, but he can tell she means "more," and he helps her fly, over and over, in the churning, rhythmic ocean that seems alive, until her brown shoulders are brick red and burning.

They lie on separate towels, under an almond tree that grows at the edge of the beach. The ocean evaporates off their skin. Occasionally they speak. The clouds are rolling in, their end-of-day routine as the island warms up, which changes the wind and currents. A pelican wanders the shoreline—great, baggy beak tucked into its neck—looking for small fish.

"Marcus"—she can't not ask this any longer—"why are you with me?"

Instead of a direct reply, he counters with his own question. "Why would I not want to be with you? You're pretty, gentle, and as sweet as the candies you cook up every morning."

She is silent, grasping sand in the palms of her tense hands. His warm, damp hand stills her, then slides the wet, tangled hair off her oily forehead and back into place. It's a gesture that reminds her of her mother. She can't turn easily to look at him; she half-sits and rolls to her right side.

"I have a brother who was born with a harelip," he continues. "Why him and not me?" The sun filtering past the almond tree branches and wide leaves makes a patchwork of dancing light across his lithe body. "I don't know if anyone knows one hundred percent why they are with someone, especially if they are in it for the right reasons. Can you accept that outside of the obvious physical attraction I feel for you and the admiration I have for you, I really don't know what else is in there? Right now, all I know is that no other woman I have been with has ever wanted to ride a board on her stomach like that, with so much joy, till she almost cooked herself." He turns his head and smiles. "The sun's going, looks like the waves picked up a bit again. Wanna go back in?"

She is stiff, but stands and smiles back. Such a simple thing to make him care. She never imagined it could be so easy.

Thursday/*jueves*

Vinegar in the milk to curdle, then the boiling of milk, and the addition of sugar and vanilla. Stirring to avoid sticking. When she sees the bottom of the pan, Delight knows the *manjar* is ready.

She needs no recipe to glance at, but somewhere in the kitchen is a small box with a yellowed card that says to remove the *manjar* from the fire. The sweet milk candy has been made by her family for so long, the directions refer to fire cooking. As Delight removes the pan and continues to stir till it softens, she hears her *abuelita*: "No matter how much you want to rush, Alegría, you must be patient. You rush, you risk losing the whole batch. And you will never be able to afford to start a new one. So keep life out of the *cocina*. The kitchen is a sanctuary. It should remain that way, my little Delight. And you will get through anything."

When Delight came in the front door last night, late, her father was drunk on Island rum and threatened to go after Marcus for dishonoring his daughter. "He is using you, this no-good surfer. Using you. You will never see him again, and I will have to live with everything, all the dishonor." He shakes his head vigorously, which makes him almost lose his balance. "You must see him *no más!*"

Delight does what she always does, tries to turn her head further down and away and to move past him, to make it to the dark, safe shadows of her room with its metal bolt. But she is not quick enough this time.

"*¡Puta!*" Then the pain of a slap across her mouth, the trickle of blood from skin grazing teeth. Only then does he move aside, always after he raises his daughter's blood to the surface, blood that tonight is black in the moonlight.

No clouds, and a heavy breeze off the land means she will lose Marcus to the waves today, expected to rise up to five feet. She spots two wild dogs scavenging in the heaps of trash that are building up and spilling over the plastic red trash barrels. She loves these two strays who know her by sight, and despite being in a rush, she bends to pet them. They are an odd couple, two males, one a good-size mongrel, the other a miniature Chihuahua. Always together. For a moment they tolerate her attention, then move on to the next barrel, hungry from a night of wandering.

A few houses up the street, she passes Ana's Make Over Salon. She never goes in, but looks carefully at the women walking out later in the day on her return trip home. She wonders if they share some secret she doesn't know.

After the long concrete barrier that runs alongside the road where it curves to a fork, the shop waits for her. He is there to take her boxes. And she realizes only then that she was afraid he would not be. Her father's voice is more powerful than she knew.

Her chin is in his salt-dried hand. "What happened here?"

She hesitates. "I will explain later." And they make plans to go out on a real date, as he calls it, to a local restaurant called The Spot, right on the water's edge.

Mercedes knows about her father, the whole town does. About his lust for blood at the cockfights, and his tendency to lose his temper at home. Delight's mother was killed in a car accident, but everyone knows she was racing to get away from the home. She couldn't make the sharp turn at the top of the hill across from the candy shop in the dark, and went over the cliff. That's why the barrier was erected.

Mercedes gives her one quick look and then embraces her. Nothing more needs to be said between the distant cousins. But she does council, "You got a good man now, Delight, don't let him get away."

"But he is going away. I can't stop it from happening."

"I know, I don't mean don't let him go home. Find a way to make him come back."

Delight ponders this all day, as she waits for her "real date."

At The Spot, they both order fish, and when the waiter brings out the dishes, they are suddenly swarmed with flies. Delight has never eaten outside by the beach, and doesn't know what other locals

know, that flies will swarm to fish until the sun goes down. They
have no choice but to eat while constantly slapping away at the
circling, buzzing invaders. They eat as fast as they can, working to
keep the flies from following the forks into their mouths, till the
sun, in one great globe of orange fire, disappears over the ocean's
horizon. And instantly the flies are gone, just as the waiter predicted.

"No wonder this place was empty when we first got here,"
Marcus says.

"I'm sorry, I should have known."

Marcus shakes his head. "Now we have a story to tell about our
first real date."

"You are positive all the time?"

He shrugs. "Not at work. I hate my job. I was talking to Joe
down at the surf shop. They are looking for instructors next year
and someone to run the shop off-season. I'm thinking of relocating.
How does that sound?"

Delight looks at him carefully. She has never been able to look
at anyone head on, and has always found that she can read people
better this way, from the side. They don't think she can really "see"
them, so they don't hide as much. She looks, and she sees nothing
false.

In a private spot on the empty beach, he finds his way inside her.
The finger he broke several years ago maneuvers gently around the
partially blocked entrance, and then he is in, and she is shuddering
and pulsing around him, shaking uncontrollably so he has to cradle
her as her arms flail. When she is done, she covers her face with
her hands. She is embarrassed and she is shameful. She hears her
father's voice.

Her father is not home when she gets back that night, intentionally
early. She inadvertently kicks the saint that is still unfinished and
lying in her path to the bedroom. It clatters into a wall. She picks it
up, runs her fingers all over the indentations and rough-hewn folds
of the robe. Then carries it to her room.

Friday/*viernes*

She grates pieces of coconut in a food processor, adding small streams of water into the glass bowl. Then she puts the ground coconut mixture in a dishtowel, and filters out the fiber to get the milk. This is her specialty, *cremitas de coco*, and she wants to make it today to perfection. All the strength of her soul goes into squeezing out the liquid, and all the hope of her heart goes into combining the secret list of different sugars that has been passed down for three generations. The coconut bars she will make when it hardens will be her going away gift for Marcus, who is leaving the following morning.

She puts aside a special box for him, with silver foil inside to keep them fresh, and every color ribbon she has in the shop that she brought home the day before is tied around all four sides.

At the shop, Mercedes tells them to leave after the morning rush is over. "It's your last day together. *Disfrute.* Have fun!" Marcus gives her cousin a hug and kisses both cheeks, and Mercedes squeezes Delight's hand before she leaves the shop.

Delight sits in the shade of a palm tree at María's Beach, a favorite surfing spot. Yellow butterflies flutter past. It is her turn to watch Marcus do what he loves. For several hours, interrupted by a few breaks, he skis the waves. He is so good, he can even walk across the board as it skims the water that curls under him, with the wind's help, like shavings of butter or chocolate. When he comes in to rest, he has a look she hasn't seen all week on his face. His eyes are a deeper brown, and they smile more.

"You know," he asks with a mouth full of chicken burrito, "I never asked you where the name Delight came from."

"My birth name is Alegría, which means Delight. But because my mother worked in the candy shop, lots of tourists came in, and one heard my mother say my name, and she thought it was so wonderful that my name sounds like a candy. So my mother and *abuelita* started calling me both. Today, only my father calls me Alegría."

"Well, I love it. Both names."

After lunch she tells him to close his eyes. She takes a *coco* bar from the cooler, tells him to open his mouth, and gives him a bite. "This is my favorite."

"Mmm . . . ," he says. "Mmm, it starts out hard, then sort of crumbles instantly, like fine, fine sweet sand. How'd you do that?" She smiles. "Many years of secret perfecting of the recipe."

"Delight," he says, and gives her a kiss.

Saturday / *sábado*

Saturday she doesn't cook, she goes to the farmer's market in Rincón. She shops for the week, and gets the best coconuts from Bermudez, who picks them himself from the edge of his farm, scaling the trunks with a rope and metal spikes on his shoes. But today she will go much later. She picks up two boxes, and tries to get past her father, who blocks the doorway.

"You are not going to the market. Where are you going? You disobeyed me and went out with that surfer again. You are not leaving this house."

Delight does not even look at him. She has learned how to survive. "Whatever you say, Papa." She turns, goes to her room, bolts the door, and climbs out the window that lost its grate to rust many years ago. Marcus was to pick her up at the store, in any case. It's simply a matter of walking through a neighbor's yard to the street, so her father doesn't see her out front.

Marcus is there, of course. They drive to a parking spot far down on the beach, so they can be alone. She gives him the box of *coco* bars, and tells him to open the other box. In it is the unfinished statue he had admired. "This is my father before life made him what he is. This is what I want you to know about him. You don't need to know anything else."

Marcus is quiet, turning the saint over in his hands. "I'm coming back, you know. I'll write when I hear from the surf shop, let you know when it's final."

Delight shrugs and looks out at the ocean, full of men and

women trying to feel free for a moment. She feels his sculpted arms pull her head, already close to his shoulder, down. "He won't come back," is all she hears as the ocean's roar rises and subsides.

Sunday/*domingo*

The shop is closed. There is nothing to cook. She stays in her room all day, no reason to leave it. Every reason to avoid her father. The blackbirds screech. She covers her ears.

Her father tells her almost daily that she won't be hearing, that no one will want her now. After the fourth week, she begins to wilt, like a flower stem without enough water. Mercedes has to work harder at the store, as Delight spends more time in the back room, hiding from people she knows. They whisper and shake their heads when she goes to the market. She stops making the sweets that need fresh coconut. She has done what her *abuelita* has told her not to do, she has let life into the kitchen, and everything suffers for it. She mixes the wrong ingredients some mornings, and doesn't realize till a customer winces after taking a bite of something. She goes down to María's Beach and Steps Beach and watches the surfers from afar. She feels pathetic, but unable to keep herself from looking to see if he came back and didn't tell her. She never sees anyone who looks like him.

Nine weeks pass by. It's a Tuesday, and she is at the store. She has started to accept things, and is out front, methodically working the cash register, when José, the postman, comes into the store, pushing past the line of customers to the front. He is sweating, and being a heavy man, panting.

"Delight," he says, holding out a postcard to her, "this is for you. I am sorry, I read it. I read all of them, and I can tell now that César has not been giving you the cards. So I brought this one directly to the store."

It's from Marcus, wondering why she has not responded to him or called him collect. If she still wants him to come. That he got the job and would be there in a few months' time, but that he would stay in California and look for something else if she didn't want him.

Mercedes is reading over her shoulder, and puts her hand on Delight's back. And pushes her forward. "Go into Rincón and call him. Don't go home first."

José is beaming, having done his part. Delight leaves the store, and walks to the bus stop. Then she turns, and walks home. Her father is on the front porch, carving. She walks up to him, holding out the postcard at the end of her straight arm like a policeman holds out a badge. She stops in front of the porch. She doesn't need to go any further. His face registers the flat object in her hand. She expected to see anger. Instead, his face seems to instantly age, growing new lines and valleys like his carvings. Father and daughter say nothing to each other. He looks down and continues working the cedar block. Turning away, she walks up the street. The sky above is a bright white, and over in the distance, above the treeline to the east, a corner of blue begins to peel away. She feels she is being lifted and carried, away from her father's anger and bitter loneliness, and even her *abuelita's* well-meaning but pitying advice, to a shore that is unexplored, but her own.

Her head is held as high as she can manage.

TARA L. MASIH grew up in the small harbor town of Northport, situated along the Long Island Sound. Much of her time was spent on the beaches and in the woods, and as a result her writing is often set within the framework of nature and place. Her fiction, poetry, and essays have been published in numerous literary magazines, including *Confrontation*, *Hayden's Ferry Review*, *Natural Bridge*, *New Millennium Writings*, *Red River Review*, *Night Train*, and *The Caribbean Writer*, as well as in many anthologies. Several limited edition, illustrated chapbooks featuring her flash fiction have been published by The Feral Press. Awards for her work include first place in *The Ledge Magazine*'s fiction contest, a finalist fiction grant from the Massachusetts Cultural Council, and Pushcart Prize, Best New American Voices, and Best of the Web nominations. Tara judges the intercultural essay prize for the annual Soul-Making Literary Contest, and is editor of the acclaimed *Rose Metal Press Field Guide to Writing Flash Fiction* (2009). C. W. Post College presented her with the Lou P. Bunce Creative Writing Award upon graduation, and Emerson College, where she received her MA in Writing and Publishing, awarded her with a Bookbuilders of Boston Scholarship. Tara now works as a freelance book editor in Andover, Massachusetts. Her website is www.taramasih.com.

—

To download a Reader's Guide for *Where the Dog Star Never Glows*, including a Q&A with the author, go to www.Press53.com/bioTaraLMasih.html

Cover artist **BENITA VANWINKLE** is currently a freelance instructor of photography, altered art, bookbinding, and other creative courses at Surry Community College, High Point University, and other institutions throughout the NC Triad region. She was Program Director at The Sawtooth School for Visual Art in Winston-Salem before leaving to pursue freelance teaching and her personal artistic passions. She moved to the Winston-Salem area from Atlanta, GA, where she was the college admissions director and photography instructor at The Creative Circus, a premier portfolio school.

Benita is a member of the Associated Artists of Winston-Salem where she regularly participates in gallery exhibitions and has earned awards of excellence in numerous exhibitions throughout the Southeast. Benita volunteers at many nonprofit institutions, including Forsyth Habitat for Humanity, the Children's Home of Winston-Salem, The Sawtooth School for Visual Art, and Riverwood Therapeutic Riding Center.

She graduated with her MFA from Southern Illinois University in Carbondale, IL, where she also served on the Board of Advisors for the Cinema and Photography department. She graduated from the University of Central Florida, Daytona Beach Community College (now Daytona College), and St. Petersburg Junior College (now St. Petersburg College). To see more of Benita's work, visit www.BusyBStudio.com.

A Note from the Author

This page has changed, shifted, evolved over the two-plus decades in which these stories were created. But it really began to be written on many years ago when my fourth-grade teacher, Ms. Emmanuel—who wore primary-blue eye makeup and lined her eyes in black like Cleopatra, and somehow managed to pile her long hair into a dark, towering bouffant—sat us down every day in a circle to read *Huckleberry Finn*. Her beauty, her voice, the words, the adventure, the subtext, and the simple poetry of Twain's prose started something that doesn't end here.

So, to her, and to my aunt Eleanor and my grandmother Frieda, who continually supplied me with books every gift-giving holiday, I owe a huge debt. Also to my parents ("Whatever you want to do, as long as you love it, we'll support you"); to my husband, Mike Gilligan, who loves both me and my writing, and often has to cook dinner while I make deadlines; to my writing friends who provide that necessary support only writers know how to give to each other: Mary Slechta, Katheryn Laborde, Kathy Aponick, Helena Minton, Dan Pritchard, Sue Williams, Kathy Handley, and Stace Budzko. To my faithful cheerleaders, who read all my work and attend readings and say nice things, and who are so talented in their own pursuits: Lyn Pinezich, Nikki Endo, and Mary Lou Wilshaw-Watts.

Many folks have their fingerprints all over this book's manuscript. Thanks to editors and teachers Stratis Haviaras, Kathy Collins, Chris Noël, and Gwen Moore; writers Tom Miller, Mary Slechta, Katheryn Laborde, Kathy Aponick, and Mike Hartnett. To my mother, Sandra Masih, and my husband, both good editors in their own right, and Bob Padykula, who read and commented on early drafts. Thanks to all the blurbers who found time to read this manuscript, despite their own tight schedules. And to the following mentors for their encouragement: Joan and John Digby; Lisa Borders (who is a font of publishing wisdom and madly generous with it all); and the late Jim Randall (Jim, I hope you are still feeding the pigeons); to Rick Bass for his writing which inspires and for his early support, and to the talented writer Grace Dane Mazur—for her support and graciousness, a special thanks. And a shout out to Grub Street, which provided a much-needed sense of community.

But mostly, thank you, Kevin Watson. I couldn't be more pleased with the warmth, professionalism, wisdom, enthusiasm, and sharp editing you continually provide. Press 53 was the ideal home for this book.

T.L.M.

CPSIA information can be obtained at www.ICGtesting.com
Printed in the USA
BVOW03s1956160315

391947BV00001B/7/P